Lily Quench
and the
MAGICIANS' PYRAMID

Natalie Jane Prior lives in Brisbane, Australia with her husband, daughter and two long-haired dachshunds. She worked as a librarian before becoming a full-time author and has since written a number of books for children and young adults including the fantastic *Lily Quench* series.

Books by Natalie Jane Prior

Lily Quench
and the
MAGICIANS' PYRAMID

NATALIE
JANE
PRIOR

Illustrated by Janine Dawson

PUFFIN

PUFFIN BOOKS

Published by the Penguin Group
Penguin Books Ltd, 80 Strand, London WC2R 0RL, England
Penguin Group (USA) Inc., 375 Hudson Street, New York, New York 10014, USA
Penguin Group (Canada), 10 Alcorn Avenue, Toronto, Ontario, Canada M4V 3B2
(a division of Pearson Penguin Canada Inc.)
Penguin Ireland, 25 St Stephen's Green, Dublin 2, Ireland (a division of Penguin Books Ltd)
Penguin Group (Australia), 250 Camberwell Road,
Camberwell, Victoria 3124, Australia (a division of Pearson Australia Group Pty Ltd)
Penguin Books India Pvt Ltd, 11 Community Centre,
Panchsheel Park, New Delhi – 110 017, India
Penguin Group (NZ), cnr Airborne and Rosedale Roads, Albany,
Auckland 1310, New Zealand (a division of Pearson New Zealand Ltd)
Penguin Books (South Africa) (Pty) Ltd, 24 Sturdee Avenue,
Rosebank, Johannesburg 2196, South Africa

Penguin Books Ltd, Registered Offices: 80 Strand, London WC2R 0RL, England

www.penguin.com

First published in Australia and New Zealand by Hodder Headline Australia Pty Ltd 2003
Published in Great Britain in Puffin Books 2005

1

British Library Cataloguing in Publication Data
A CIP catalogue record for this book is available from the British Library

ISBN 0–141–31864–3

www.lilyquench.com

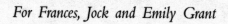

For Frances, Jock and Emily Grant

Some Old Friends...

Lily Quench

Last of the dragon-slaying Quenches of Ashby, Lily and her friend, Queen Dragon, drove the Black Count's army out of Ashby and restored the lost prince, Lionel, to his throne. Lily later rediscovered her family's secret weapon (metal-eating Quenching Drops), rebuilt Ashby's fortunes by discovering the Treasure of Mote Ely, and is trying to track down the location of the magical Eye Stones to prevent them being used in an invasion from the Black Empire.

Queen Dragon

Sinhault Fierdaze (known to her friends as Queen Dragon) is a three thousand year old crimson dragon, the size of a four storey house. When not in Ashby she lives in a volcano, where she keeps a stockpile of treasure to snack on when she's hungry (dragons eat metal).

King Lionel of Ashby

The son of King Alwyn the last, who was killed at the Siege of Ashby during the Black Count's invasion.

Queen Evangeline of Ashby

Born Evangeline Bright, and a former supporter of the Black Count, Evangeline helped drive the Count's forces from Ashby and later married the king.

Mr Hartley

The Minister of the Ashby Church, Mr Hartley was driven out of Ashby as a young man by the Black Count's army. Mr Hartley helped Lily restore the lost prince, Lionel, to the throne of Ashby.

Dr Angela Hartley

A former slave of the Black Count, Angela was the foster mother of his son, Gordon, for many years. She was rescued and reunited with her husband and has returned to live and work in Ashby.

Sir Wilibald (formerly Captain) Zouche

As Governor of Ashby for the Black Count, Captain Zouche was feared for his loud voice and dreadful temper. He was sent to work in the grommet factory, where his experiences led to a change of heart.

Sir Jason Pearl

The son of the Keeper of Ashby Thicket, Jason rode Queen Dragon to victory during the Battle of Ashby Church. For his bravery, he was made Royal Chamberlain and a member of King Lionel's Council.

Murdo

Born two hundred years in the past, Murdo joined the army Gordon was training at the Castle of Mote Ely, and was feared as a cruel bully. Murdo was pushed down a well by his brother during a quarrel and badly injured. He was brought forward into Lily's time so his life could be saved.

King Dragon

Thousands of years ago, during the Great War of the Dragons at Dragon's Downfall in the Black Mountains, Queen Dragon's long lost fiancé led a small party of dragons through an Eye Stone in search of help. He has never returned.

One

THE BUBBLING POOL

The pool steamed like a cup of hot soup on a winter's morning, peaty brown, and full of slow-moving bubbles. From time to time the bubbles broke the surface and a sulphur smell rose up on the cool air. A sedgy wilderness stretched as far as the eye could see. There were no trees or hills, just clumps of tussocky grass intercut with tiny streams, all seemingly running nowhere under a lowering sky.

A strange shape like a pointing finger was

reflected in the water. It was carved out of some kind of black rock, with a hole bored through the middle. The surface of the water darkened as a girl's face appeared, reflected beside the stone. It was small and resolute, with neat features framed by a halo of soft, long hair and a winged silver helmet.

The girl looked carefully at the reflection of the pointed stone. A huge drift of steam went puffing over the pool, momentarily obscuring it, then something large and red loomed up behind her.

'Do you think it's an Eye Stone, Lily?'

Lily Quench turned to the enormous dragon standing behind her. Sinhault Fierdaze, known affectionately as Queen Dragon, was an old friend and battle companion with whom she had been through many adventures. Lily trusted Queen Dragon more than anyone else on earth. Though neither of them had expected to find the mysterious stone here, it was, in a sense, the reason for their journey. They had come to the wastelands of the north to try and find the location of every Eye Stone in existence, so that they could close them all off forever.

'I think so,' said Lily cautiously. 'It looks just like the Eye Stone at Dragon's Downfall in the Black Mountains.' She bit her lip in thought. 'Do you think it's working?'

'Probably,' said Queen Dragon. 'The question is, why would anyone want to build one here?'

Lily didn't reply. The truth was, she didn't know, and it troubled her. Somewhere beyond the ring of stones was their destination, a cluster of pyramids inhabited by the magicians who had built the Eye Stones long ago. Eye Stones were magical doorways, a way of travelling from place to place and time to time. They had been fashioned by bad and dangerous magic, and Lily knew it was perilous to get too close to them. But it was also true that she could not learn much from looking at a reflection. That was the problem. A dozen paces away to the west an identical stone stood pointing like a finger at the lowering sky, and beyond it was yet another, just visible on the edge of her vision. To the east, more stones stretched away across the sedgy landscape to the horizon, strung out in a circle like a necklace of teeth. It was a magical fenceline, a definite boundary. Once they crossed it, there was no saying what would happen or who they might meet.

A fat cold droplet fell on Lily's forehead. She looked up. The sky was black with clouds and there was a sharp tang in the air as if a downpour was heading their way.

'Let's make camp,' suggested Queen Dragon. 'That way we can think about what to do next. In any case, we don't want to fly closer to the pyramids before nightfall. I wonder how far we are from them?' She shook out her wings and arched them to form a sort of red leathery tent. Lily went inside and moments later, the rain started pouring down, splashing and sizzling against Queen Dragon's scales.

Lily started to unpack. She spread out a groundsheet, unrolled her sleeping bag and put out a billy to catch some rainwater. As she did, something buzzed past her ear. It was a small black fly.

'Get lost! Shoo!' The fly buzzed aggressively past again. Lily flapped her hand in front of her face, but it refused to go away. It alighted on her hand, then on her cheek, each time zipping off before Lily could slap and squash it. There was a second's silence. Lily cringed and looked around her. A moment later she felt something crawling on the back of her neck.

'Shoo! Shoo! Get lost!' Lily threw herself forward and rolled across the groundsheet. The fly zoomed past her ear and then she heard it coming back, heading straight for her face. Lily yelled, jumped up and ran out from under Queen Dragon's sheltering wing.

'Lily!' Queen Dragon cried out, too late. The dark shadow of the Eye Stone loomed up in front of her, its hole whirling like a maelstrom. Lily had a single second to realise how stupid she had been. Then, before she could turn around and flee, there was a tumbling, sucking sensation and she landed with a heavy thump on some wet grass.

Lily lay sprawled on the ground, confused and breathless. Travelling by Eye Stone was always a dizzying experience, and she had landed unexpectedly hard and fast. Her fingers were snagged in the same kind of tufty, sedgy grass she had been standing on a few moments earlier. It was raining heavily, and water was soaking through her thick woollen dress and knitted tights.

I've scarcely moved, Lily thought. *This is exactly the same place I was at before. Why, there's the ring of Eye Stones, and there's Queen Dragon—oh!* Lily's heart gave a lurch of fright. She sat up, her pulse racing. Rising in front of her, out of the mist of rain, was a gigantic shadowy building. Its stones were set at an angle and were dark with water; they rose to an unseen point somewhere in the drizzle overhead. There were no windows. The single door was set into the sloping face at the top of a flight of steps. It was framed by a massive stone lintel, on which was carved a picture of a gigantic eye.

A moment ago, the pyramid had simply not been there. It was as if a magical curtain had been pulled back, making the invisible visible to Lily's eyes. The eye had the same eyelashes she had seen on a mysterious well on the Island of Skansey, a well that had also turned out to be an Eye Stone. Lily felt small and terrified. She felt sure the horrible thing was watching her every move.

She called out. 'Queen Dragon! What should we do now?'

Her voice faded thinly into the cold air. There was no reply. Still not understanding what had happened, Lily turned to Queen Dragon and, for the first time, fully realised what the Eye Stone had done.

Queen Dragon was standing by the Eye Stone, her wings still arched over Lily's abandoned campsite. But she was now on the *opposite side* of the bubbling pool. The Eye Stone had sucked Lily through to the inside of the stone circle. Lily saw Queen Dragon's mouth moving, calling her name, and then she saw Queen Dragon start to waddle towards the stone. Immediately Lily realised what her friend was going to do. She waved her hands frantically and shouted, 'No, Queen Dragon! Don't do it! Stop!'

But Lily's cries were useless. Queen Dragon could neither see nor hear her, and nor could she see the magicians' pyramid, so perilously close. Lily flung herself at the Eye Stone and beat her fists on it. She flapped her arms and screamed, to no avail. Queen Dragon lifted her claw to strike between her scales and draw the drops of dragon's blood that Lily knew could control the Eye Stone's magic. In desperation, Lily tried to poke her hands through the hole in the stone.

A black force suddenly shot out of the hole in the Eye Stone. It lifted Lily bodily off her feet and flung her backwards across the heath. She hit the ground, felt her helmet fly off her head and heard it land with a splash in a puddle; then somersaulted to a juddering halt against a rock. Lily had just enough time to realise Queen Dragon had vanished when she heard a buzzing sound close by. The fly had come back and was sitting on her arm.

Lily lifted her hand. But before she got the chance to knock it off, she felt a small sharp burning sensation and saw a thin trail of blood running down her wrist. Then the sky started turning giddily above her head and she fainted.

Two

A THIEF IN THE NIGHT

In the town of Ashby Water, it was night. Soft moonlight washed over the buildings and rippled on the water of the Ashby Canal. An owl hooted—for now that the town's gardens had been replanted the birds were coming back—but otherwise everything was normal. A choir practice had just finished in the Ashby church. In the hospital, the nurses went on their evening rounds. One patient lay awake, staring sullenly at the ceiling; but if he was plotting anything, he kept it to himself. His name was Murdo, and he did not belong in Ashby or even in the time in which he found himself.

In the garden of the little house belonging to Lily Quench, Mr Thwaites, the head gardener of the Ashby Botanic Gardens, finished doing the watering for her. He turned off the hose and walked away home. A light burned in his kitchen. His wife and foster son, Tom, were sitting up for him, and there was a hot supper waiting on the table. Whistling cheerfully, Mr Thwaites walked up the gravel path and let himself in. The owl, which had been perched on the ridge-capping, swivelled its head and soared silently away.

It flew over the beehive-shaped dragon house where Queen Dragon stayed during her visits to Ashby, and the churchyard where Lily's grandmother Ursula Quench lay buried. Then it soared on over castle and town to Ashby Thicket. In the royal bedchamber in Ashby Castle, King Lionel heard it hooting and looked up from his book. Queen Evangeline, expecting a baby and needing her rest, was already asleep beside him, but Lionel's day had been a busy one, and he was trying to relax before turning out the light.

Mad Brian Quench pulled his fireproof cape over his head and approached the bottomless cave (the king read, breathlessly). *He knew that in its depths lay untold wealth, stolen from every hold and castle east of the Black Mountains. But Brian cared naught for treasure. He had come to save the lives of the thirty-seven innocent children who lay within; children who had been stolen from their parents by an insane dragon, whose slavering jaws even now waited to crush him to a bloody pulp—*

WAA-AAR! WAA-AAR! WAA-AAR! WAA-AAR! WAA-AAR! WAA-AAR!

A deafening noise rocked the castle. Bells rang. Sirens wailed. Lights snapped on all over the building and booted feet were heard running in the castle corridors. Queen Evangeline woke with a start, wide-eyed and shaking. The king shot out of bed and was half into his dressing gown when there was a loud pounding on the door.

'Declare yourself!' shouted the king. He grabbed his sceptre from beside the bed and wielded it menacingly. The door flew open and a small blond boy stumbled in. It was the Royal Chamberlain, Sir Jason Pearl.

'Your Majesty!' he gasped. 'Intruders! In the old dungeons!'

'Intruders!' Queen Evangeline rolled out of bed and started shoving on her fluffy slippers. 'Lionel! *The treasure!*'

The king dashed out into the corridor. Terrified people were running in and out of their bedrooms, afraid that the invasion everybody feared had come. Lionel shouted to them to go back to bed, but nobody listened. The queen grabbed a torch from her bedside table. She had never turned her back on danger and was not going to start now.

'Go back to bed, Evie!' shouted the king. 'It's not safe! Stay upstairs!'

'Not likely!' retorted Evangeline, struggling to tie her dressing gown over her pregnant tummy. She caught up with Lionel and Jason at the end of the passage and ran with them down the main stairs. Outside, the castle bailey raced with searchlights. Lionel paused to shout an order to the captain of the royal guard, then cut across to the castle gatehouse. At an obscure door in the guardroom, the royal party stopped. It was the entrance to the former Ashby Castle dungeons.

Lionel knew them well. He had once been locked in them himself and threatened with torture by Miss Moldavia, who had schemed to rule Ashby and tried to force him to marry her. He had met Lily there and discovered his destiny as king. But the dungeons were too horrible to remain in use after Lionel's coronation. By his royal decree, all locks, bars and torture implements used in the Black Count's time had been destroyed, and the dungeons converted to treasure vaults, especially built to store the matchless Treasure of Mote Ely.

'Turn off the alarm!' shouted the king, but no one seemed to hear him. Lionel rattled through a gigantic bunch of keys and opened the door. He ran down a staircase into the vaults, unlocked a second door made of metal, and stopped at an electric gate and guardpost. Evangeline grabbed the bars and rattled them like a prisoner.

'Where are all the guards?' she demanded. Lionel found the key and grimly opened the gate. As they stepped past the guardpost, the lights around them flickered. Evangeline caught a glimpse of a figure in a long hooded cape, then a groaning sigh went through the electrical system and the entire castle was plunged into darkness.

'Hey! Turn the lights back on!' yelled Jason. Evangeline whipped her torch out of her pocket and darted after the fleeing figure.

'Come back, Evie!' shouted the king. 'You'll hurt yourself!'

'He's getting away!' The queen lumbered forward through the darkness, her tiny light bouncing off the whitewashed walls of the old dungeon. The intruder ran around a corner and down a few steps. Evangeline heard a door slam across the corridor and lost precious seconds opening it; she ran through the old torture chamber, now an office, dodging desks and filing cabinets. Her quarry paused at the other end to throw a chair at her. Evangeline ducked it, losing a slipper; she grabbed a wastepaper basket and hurled it back, but it bounced off the door as it closed.

'Come back, you robber!' she yelled breathlessly. 'Keep your hands off our treasure!' She wrenched open the door and ran around a corner, almost knocking herself out on a door which should not have been open. It was one of the vaults. The lock had been wrenched off and the latch snapped. Evangeline saw a light inside, as if someone was shining a torch over the canvas bags of coins and jewels on the shelves.

The thief started back from the shelves, a sack in his right hand, a lantern in his left. Its beam swept across Evangeline's face, momentarily dazzling her. For the first time she caught a glimpse of his hooded face and saw a mask over his nose and mouth. With a crash, he dropped the sack and lunged at her. The queen's hands closed on his cloak and they tussled together in the doorway.

'Let go!' shouted the thief in a muffled voice. Evangeline saw his eyes, furious, yet frightened, above his mask. She kicked out at his shins with her remaining slipper and shouted frantically for help.

'Lionel! Jason! Come quickly!'

'Where are you? What's happening?'

Evangeline heard the others blundering in the darkness along the outside passage. She tightened her grip on the intruder's cloak, but he was stronger than she was, and she was heavy and clumsy because of her baby. Suddenly the intruder gave her a vicious shove. Evangeline gave a loud cry and staggered backwards. One of her feet skidded on some coins from the broken money bag and she hit the floor with a mighty thud. The intruder hurled his lantern across the room and was gone in a flash. Evangeline felt a sharp pain in her back, a spinning in her head, and then fainted.

In the throne room of Ashby Castle, King Lionel summoned an emergency meeting of his three remaining councillors, Sir Jason Pearl, Sir Wilibald Zouche and Mr Hartley, Minister of the Ashby Church.

'Gentlemen,' he said grimly, 'tonight has proved we live in perilous times. The Queen of Ashby has been attacked in her own castle. The Treasure of Mote Ely has almost been lost. An unknown intruder, an enemy of Ashby, has successfully penetrated our securest vaults. If not for the queen's intervention, his plans might have succeeded. He might have blown up the castle and killed every one of us. Or he might have stolen the treasure we need to rebuild our towns, to feed our people, to protect Ashby in case of a war.

'Tonight, we must look at two questions. First, how did the intruder get into the vaults? And second, what is his or her identity? Sir Jason, you have the plans. Will you please report?'

'Your Majesty.' Sir Jason stood up and bowed to the king. 'As you can see on this plan of the dungeons, there is no entrance to the treasure vaults except the one in the gatehouse. Every vault is triple locked with alarms, safety doors and trip switches. Eight armed guards work on every shift. Until tonight, I would have said the vaults were impregnable.'

'So would I,' said the king. He looked at the plan and bit his finger thoughtfully. 'There's something missing from this map, Jason. There used to be a secret tunnel to Ashby Church. Lily's grandmother used it to rescue me from the Siege of Ashby when I was a little boy. Does anyone know if it's been sealed off?'

'As far as I know it hasn't been,' said Mr Hartley. 'Lily used it too, just before the Battle of Ashby Church, but I don't think anyone else knew about it. The entrance is in the church crypt under Matilda Drakescourge's tomb.'

'Securely locked?'

'Always. There's a new iron gate and I have the only key.'

'We'll still check it out.' The king made notes on a piece of paper. 'The guards who were on duty are being questioned now. It seems they were all playing Scrabble in the mess room, and were locked in by the intruder. As far as we know, not one of them saw a thing.'

'Did the queen see the intruder's face?' asked Sir Wilibald.

'He was masked. Evangeline thinks he was a boy or young man, but she couldn't be sure.' The king picked up a broken lantern and a heavy grey woollen cloak. 'Whoever he was, he was carrying this lantern and wearing this cloak. They're rather unusual. At the moment, they're our only clues.'

He laid the items on the table. The three councillors looked at them for a moment in silence.

'That's a miner's lantern,' said Mr Hartley. He reached across the table and picked it up. The lantern was small and square, with a round lamp and a metal handle. A number was stamped on the side: XIII. 'I've seen these many times, when I've visited the Black Mountains. The number means it comes from mine number thirteen.'

Across the table, Sir Wilibald cleared his throat. 'That cloak,' he said gruffly. 'It's military issue. When I was in the Black Count's army the Black Squads wore them over their greatcoats when they were on guard duty.'

The room went suddenly very still.

It was not an empty silence, for it was filled with memories. Sir Wilibald, former Governor of Ashby for the Black Count, was remembering his youth in the Black Mountains, and the day he had left for the invasion of Ashby. Mr Hartley was thinking of the invasion, too. In his mind's eye he saw Geoffrey Quench, Lily's father, who had died with King Lionel's father in a moat full of flame. He thought of his own wife, Angela, who had been dragged screaming from Ashby Castle and thrown into a slave truck, his long hopeless searches in the Black Mountains, the cold and the misery, the despair in the miners' eyes. And Lionel was thinking of Gordon. Gordon, who had become Black Count when his father had died at Dragon's Downfall; Gordon, who had lost his father's empire to General Sark and taken refuge in the past. *Remember this*, Gordon had said to him. *I will come back to our own time and claim my father's empire. But when I come, I will send Ashby a warning first. My father always gave his enemies a chance to surrender before he attacked them. And like him, I am a man of my word.*

A chill seemed to fill the room, as if it had blown in from the very heart of the Black Empire. Lionel picked up and mechanically folded the cloak, but still no one spoke. At last a gentle tap sounded on the throne room door.

'Your Majesty.' A footman entered with a folded paper on a silver salver and knelt before the king. 'This was found on the floor of the treasure vaults.'

Lionel took the paper. He read it silently, then tossed it on the council table.

The message read simply, *I have arrived*. And beneath the writing was a rough drawing of a hand clenched in a fist.

Three

THE MAGICIANS' BANQUET

Lily lay prisoner in a dark place. She did not know where she was or how she had come there. Her head was full of dreadful dreams of people screaming and laughing, of black shapes and echoes that she could not understand. Horrible things ran at her, shadows loomed and chattered. Disembodied voices whispered in her ear and told her she was worthless.

You think you're a Quench?

Everyone knows you're just a Cornstalk in fancy dress.

This quest is going to fail. You knew that even before you got here. I know what you're thinking. You're scared...

You're a failure, Lily. A failure, a failure, a failure. You're frightened about this quest. I know you are. How could you possibly hope to take on the magicians? Better give in...better give in...better give in...

—*No!*—

Failure...failure...failure... Better give in...

—*No!*— Somehow, Lily managed to reply. — *You're trying to trick me. Who do you think you are? You've got no power over me! I know who I am and what I'm worth!*—

The thought flew out and shattered the attacking shapes. At once the darkness vanished. Lily wrinkled her nose, crinkled her eyes, and opened them.

She was lying on a sort of high, overstuffed sofa. It was covered with shiny material that scratched her cheek, and everything smelled peculiar, like particularly nasty incense. Lamps in brackets cast a dim light around the walls and a fire burned in a central hearth. It took Lily a moment to realise there was no chimney. The fire gave off neither warmth nor smoke, and the room was very cold.

Lily sat up slowly. Even the furniture looked odd. The sofa she was sitting on had clawed feet, like a black panther, and the chair backs were carved crocodile heads. There was a table that looked like a chained bat with outstretched wings. As Lily looked around, her memory of what had happened slowly returned. She had been lured through the Eye Stone and attacked in front of the pyramid. Which meant... Lily looked up at the ceiling and saw that the stone walls were very high and slightly sloping towards the top. If her guess was right, she was now *inside* the pyramid.

And the table she had thought was a bat was, in fact, a chained dragon.

As Lily watched, a piece of folded paper appeared in the dragon's mouth. She reached over and gingerly took it out. It unfolded in her hands and she read the following message:

WELCOME, VISITOR! PLEASE BE OUR GUEST AT DINNER. WE HOPE WE HAVE PROVIDED FOR

ALL YOUR ΠEEDS AΠD LOOK FORWARD TO THE PLEASURE OF YOUR COΠPAΠY, VERY SHORTLY.

The note disappeared like smoke between Lily's fingers.

Lily hopped down off the sofa. A dress and shoes, made of cloth of gold and obviously just her size, had materialised on a chair off to the side. Beside them stood a washstand with a fluffy towel and a silver basin filled with lavender scented bubbles. Lily swirled her hand in the water. It was unpleasantly lukewarm, and as the bubbles parted for a moment under the motion of her hand, something caught her eye on the bottom of the basin. Lily recoiled. A raised figure of a hooded snake had been sculpted into the silver and seemed to move as the water rippled over it.

No matter how dirty she was, there was no way she was going to wash in *that*. Lily wiped her hand on her skirt and looked into the mirror which backed the washstand. The face that stared back at her looked rather older than Lily knew she really was, with hair more golden and eyes far bluer than they should have been. She suddenly felt impatient and annoyed at all the tricks. *Who do they think I am?* she thought. *If they expect me to be flattered, they must think I'm either awfully vain or very stupid.* The thought gave Lily a little courage. Then a voice spoke unexpectedly behind her, and she whirled around.

'You're awake at last. Are you feeling any better?'

A strange woman was sitting on the sofa. She had dark eyes and fair hair pulled back into several long loopy plaits. She was quite pretty, though not as pretty as Lily suspected she thought she was herself.

'Don't you like the dress I chose for you? I think it's such a lovely one. Gold seemed just your colour. But perhaps I was wrong.'

'The dress is lovely.' Lily decided there was nothing for it but to tell the truth. 'I prefer my own things.'

'So I see.' A faint smirk showed on the woman's face. Lily looked down at her dress. It was shabby and old and, since Lily had grown quite a bit recently, its hem was now too short. But Lily knew it was like that because for so long there had been no money in Ashby to buy new things. She did not think there was any shame in being poor, and in any case, she was hardly going to take her best clothes on a quenching expedition.

'I'm Quin,' said the woman. 'May I ask your name?'

'Lily. Lily… Cornstalk.'

'Welcome, Lily. May I ask what brings you here?'

Lily hesitated. Cornstalk had been her mother's name, so she had not exactly been lying, but instinct told her that now was not the time to say why she was here. She was still searching for an excuse when Quin continued, 'My colleague, Roger, was very much surprised to see you arrive. This is such a lonely place we rarely receive visitors. Roger thought perhaps you might be a magician yourself.' Again Lily remained silent. Quin said softly, 'You see, Lily, dragons are very dangerous animals. It would take a powerful magic to bring one under control. My other colleague, Joscelin, is something of an expert and even he took quite some time to bring yours through the barrier.'

Lily gasped. 'Queen Dragon's here? Where?'

'Queen Dragon? Is that her name? Yes, she's here. I promise you'll see her shortly.' Quin stood up. 'It's almost time for dinner. Would you like to come with me?'

A door appeared in the wall where there had been none before. Lily nodded reluctantly. She followed Quin out and they walked on together for a long way, turning several corners and going down some stairs.

At length they stopped in front of a pair of enormous inlaid doors. Quin spoke a word Lily did not catch and the doors swung inwards. Lily stepped over the threshold and gasped.

She had entered a long narrow room with a vaulted ceiling and tapestries hung around the walls. A table stood on a central dais and was set for a meal; two men in long robes were already seated there. But Lily scarcely gave either of them a glance, for her attention was entirely directed upwards. The whole ceiling was covered with the most amazing mosaic that was almost completely made of gold.

The mosaic glittered in the lamplight as if it were alive. It was covered with pictures of dozens of animals, magical animals such as one might normally encounter in a book. There was a griffin and two unicorns, a manticore with a man's head and the body of a lion, and a green winged horse with a wild expression in its eyes. The colours were so bright and fierce and the pictures so accurate the creatures looked like they were going to jump out at her. Worst of all, at the very end of the room was a stunning portrait of a red dragon, caught in the act of breathing fire on some unseen victim. When she looked at it, Lily's left arm began to throb alarmingly—a sure sign that danger was at hand.

It was Queen Dragon to the life. Lily could not believe that whoever had made the mosaic had not seen her in the flesh, though where or when this had happened she could not guess. Lily dragged her eyes away from the mosaic dragon and became aware that the magician at the end of the table, a man with black, silver-streaked hair and a swarthy complexion, was staring at her intently. And he was looking not at her face, but at her left arm.

Ever since she'd been a baby, Lily's elbow had been covered with a small patch of scaly skin. All members of the Quench family had it, though compared to others Lily's scaly patch was very small. But in a recent adventure on the battlements of Mote Ely Castle, a bucket of burning hot dragon's blood had been tipped over Lily's head. Her fireproof cape had protected her from the worst of it, but where the dragon's blood had touched it, Lily's skin had changed. Her right hand and left forearm were now coated with a shiny covering of soft silvery scales.

As Lily watched, the magician at the end of the table thrust his right arm out of its sleeve. Like hers, it was covered with scales, but the skin was purple and twisted, like decomposing chicken flesh, gone hard and dead. It was so horrible it made Lily feel sick just to look at it.

'I see you, too, are a dragon slayer,' the magician said.

'Lily Cornstalk,' said Quin, 'this is Joscelin. And my other colleague, Roger.'

Lily bowed faintly. She did not know what to say. Her whole forearm burned like it was on fire, and for a moment there was a rushing in her ears as if she were about to pass out. Her left hand went instinctively into her pocket and folded around something she had put there back in Ashby: a small filigree box, given to her as a gift on a previous quest. Before Lily realised what she was doing, its lid flipped back under the pressure of her fingers and she had brought it out and lifted it close to her face.

A strong, sweet perfume like roses and hyacinths rose up from inside the box. Lily's spirits soared. She no longer felt frightened, for she was smelling a magical flower that had bloomed unchanged from the very beginning of the world. It had been cut for her in the Drihtan's garden on Skellig Lir for such a time as this. It was a moon rose, as pink and perfect as it had been on the day it had first blossomed.

Quin hissed and Roger looked uncomfortable. Suddenly, there was the sound of a chair being shoved aside and the box was grabbed from her hands. 'No!' Lily cried, but Joscelin had already slammed it shut and hurled it into the fireplace. The box hit the stone wall at the back of the hearth and bounced off. A roaring sheet of white flame shot up from it. Quin hurried down from the dais. She retrieved the box with some fire tongs and gingerly carried it at arm's length back to the table. Lily snatched it up and put it into her pocket.

'Really, Joscelin,' Quin said, shaking. 'I don't know what you were thinking. Imagine the stink it would make if it burned.'

Joscelin glowered. 'There's no power in it, anyway.'

'Not for you, at any rate,' said Roger snidely.

'That's enough from you.' Quin sat down and shook out her napkin. 'Well. Shall we eat, everybody? Roast saffron peacock!'

She clapped her hands loudly and immediately a peacock with all its feathers appeared on a golden plate in front of her. Across the table Roger called for snails. A great dish of them arrived, all in their shells, with a little hook to fish them out. As Lily watched, Joscelin's plate filled up with an evil dark-coloured soup. He picked up his spoon and looked at her, impassive as before.

'What would you like, Lily?'

Lily considered. She was so hungry she realised she must have been unconscious for a long time.

'Roast lamb,' she said, and added quickly, 'on an ordinary plate, please.' She did not think she was up to solid gold crockery.

As the words left her mouth the dinner appeared on a white china plate, the roast meat swimming lushly in gravy with crispy roast potatoes, baby carrots and asparagus off to the side. There was even a tiny jug of mint sauce to go with it. A moment later a crystal glass appeared, accompanied by a jug of iced water. Lily poured some out for herself, and tucked in.

The first mouthful was an unpleasant surprise. It looked like a carrot, but it certainly did not taste like one, and despite the steam rising up from the plate, it was barely warm. Lily cast a sidewards glance towards her dinner companions, but they were all intent on their meals. She ventured a mouthful of lamb and found it no better than the vegetables. In fact, it was all she could do not to spit it out.

Lily soldiered on as best she could, but there seemed little difference from one type of food to the next. Furthermore, though her stomach seemed to be filling up she felt unsatisfied, as if she hadn't eaten at all. About halfway through the meal dessert arrived with a thump on the table in front of her: a large slice of apple pie, smothered in whipped cream and dusted with icing sugar. Lily put down her knife and fork and pushed it away. The apples she grew in her orchard on the Island of Skansey were among the best in the world. She had no intention of spoiling her palate with these.

The magicians continued eating, barely speaking or even looking at each other. Meanwhile, a small crystal tumbler had appeared on the table in front of each of them. Lily wondered what it was for. At the end of the first course, Joscelin put down his soup spoon. He reached into his robes and retrieved an ornate silver flask from some inner pocket.

Quin and Roger sat up expectantly. A sickening stench filled the room as Joscelin unstoppered the flask. Lily gagged and covered her mouth. There was something dead and rotten about the smell, and it made her want to be sick.

Joscelin poured three careful measures of an evil-looking potion and handed the glasses to his colleagues.

'To us. Long life and health.' He raised the glass in a toast.

'To us,' echoed Quin and Roger. There was the ghost of a grimace on Roger's face and a set look on Quin's as they tossed the liquid down. Then from somewhere outside the pyramid, Lily heard a loud and bloodcurdling cry. It was unmistakably a dragon in pain...

FOUR

THE OBSERVATORY

Lily jumped to her feet. 'What was that?'
Quin calmly picked up a peach which
had appeared on her plate. She peeled its
skin off and started cutting
it up into tiny pieces.
Roger looked at
Joscelin, then tilted
the rim of his crystal
glass towards him.

'Some kind of
animal,' said Joscelin.

'There are all sorts of strange night noises around here.'

'It wasn't an animal.' Fear for Queen Dragon made Lily bold. She took a few steps towards Joscelin and clenched her fists. 'It was a dragon. It was Queen Dragon. I know she's here. Where have you put her?'

Joscelin's dark eyes burned. He glared down at Lily along his beak of a nose, and his fingers tightened around the glass until the knuckles went white under the purple. Lily felt her arm tingle furiously, but she did not care. She opened her mouth to demand again where Queen Dragon was. But before she could say anything, Roger hastily pushed back his chair.

'I think Lily's tired.' He laid his hand on Lily's shoulder and gave it a warning squeeze. 'Lily? Perhaps you'd like to go back to your room?'

Lily opened her mouth to say no. Then her eye fell once more on the mosaic dragon. Common sense kicked in: she was not going to find Queen Dragon by arguing here. Silently, she curtsied to the other magicians and followed Roger out of the room.

'Let me give you one piece of advice, Lily,' said

Roger, as they walked away. 'While you're here, do not annoy Joscelin. I know he's a fright and a bully, but you mustn't get on the wrong side of him, you absolutely mustn't.'

'All right, I won't,' said Lily. She added, 'He scared me.'

'He scares me too,' said Roger. 'Can you imagine what he's like to live with? Nothing but doom and gloom, and then that purple hand coming out of his sleeve when you least expect it, like a rat out of a drainpipe. Oh, it's all fun here at the pyramids, I can assure you. What did you think of the dinner? It was awful, wasn't it?'

'It did taste funny,' Lily agreed. 'Not like roast lamb at all.'

'That's because it isn't real,' said Roger. 'Nothing made by magic can ever quite match up to the real thing. I used to think it tasted like sawdust held together with glue. Now, of course, I can't remember what the real stuff tastes like.' They reached a place where the passage forked. Roger stopped and smiled down at her. 'Your room's that way, Lily. Do you want to go back there? Or would you rather come with me? I thought you might like to visit my observatory.'

Lily thought of her windowless room with its strange furniture. She did not fancy the thought of going back there. 'Thank you,' she said. 'I'd like to come with you, very much.'

They walked along together for about a minute, eventually reaching a hall that sloped downwards like a ramp. Lights burned in niches in its walls, and Lily glimpsed carvings she decided she did not want to look at more closely. At the bottom of the passage was a stone door. It was made from a single enormous slab of granite, cut in two and set together so precisely that it would have been impossible to put a razor blade between the slabs.

'Quite something, isn't it?' said Roger. 'Joscelin made it. He built all the pyramids except mine, though I admit, most of the others are not as impressive as this one.' He lifted his hand and the door swung silently open.

Lily saw stars and the other pyramids standing starkly silhouetted in the moonlight. Roger was already striding down the long set of steps towards a path lined with phosphorescent gravel, his ankle-length robe billowing out behind him like a patch of night. Lily paused to watch the doors close behind her. Above her head was the great lintel with the eye that she had seen on the front of the pyramid on her arrival. The eye was shut now, but Lily somehow felt it was still watching. She shuddered, and hurried down the steps to get away from it.

Queen Evangeline of Ashby was sitting in bed with a heap of books. She felt very tired and rather depressed. That in itself was unusual, for she was normally full of enthusiasm. But after the attack in the dungeons Dr Angela Hartley had ordered her straight to bed. Since it was for the sake of her unborn baby, for once the queen hadn't tried to say no.

Evangeline liked to be busy. The worst time in her life had been the years before her marriage, when she had done nothing but sit around drinking cocktails and driving her sports car as fast as she could. Today she felt particularly unhappy about being stuck in bed because Lionel and Mr Hartley were searching the secret passage for clues about their intruder. Since she couldn't go with them, Evangeline had decided to do some research. She had spent the morning reading every old book about Ashby Castle she could find, in case one of them mentioned the secret passage. One book mentioned an abandoned drain under the moat, which had been used as an escape tunnel during a long-forgotten war, another a secret panel in the throne room (now used, Evangeline knew, as a cupboard for the royal vacuum cleaner). But about the passage leading out of the dungeons, there was not a single word.

She was just about to give up when there was a tap on the bedroom door and Lionel came in, dirty and dishevelled in an old tracksuit and sneakers. Evangeline put aside her book and sat up eagerly.

'Did you find anything?'

'I'm afraid not.' Lionel kicked off his sneakers and sat down. 'We followed the passage all the way from the castle to the church. There's a bit of damp where it goes under the old moat—I think there must be a spring there or something—but that's it. It's a horrible place. I'd forgotten how awful it was.' He was quiet a moment, and Evangeline knew he was thinking about his long-ago rescue during the Siege of Ashby. She let him be, and after a bit Lionel went on. 'The church end is completely blocked off. They've put a new iron gate on the crypt and it's very strong. Nobody could open it without a key, and nobody could possibly wriggle through the bars, even if they could get into the church without being noticed. Besides, once an intruder entered the crypt, he'd have to know how to find the passage. There's a hidden spring on Matilda Drakescourge's tomb. Unless somebody told you the secret, you'd never even know it was there.'

'Booby-trap it,' suggested Evangeline. 'Rig up a bucket of paint, so that if anyone tries to get in that way it will fall on them and we'll know who they are.'

'That's a good thought,' said Lionel, brightening. 'I'll send Mr Hartley a message straightaway. And I've got another idea. If we sprinkle the passage floor with sand, we'll be able to see footprints if anyone tries to use it. That should give us some clues as well.' As he spoke, someone knocked on the door. 'Come in!' the king called and the door opened. It was Jason Pearl.

'Why, Jason, what's the matter?' asked the queen. Jason's normally pale, eager face was white, and his blond hair was even wilder than usual. Strangest of all, he seemed lost for words. Then the queen saw the green canvas bag Jason was carrying. It was a money satchel, stamped with the royal crest and the words *Treasury of Ashby*.

Mutely, Jason handed the bag to the king. Lionel flipped back the flap. It was empty.

'I don't understand,' said the king blankly. 'I was just down there. Everything was perfectly normal. When did this happen?'

'The alarms were switched off while you and Mr Hartley were investigating,' said Jason miserably. 'We think the thief slipped in behind your back.'

'But how?' demanded Lionel. 'How could anyone get into the vaults without our knowing? There were guards on the door. The church gate was locked, the only key was in Mr Hartley's pocket!'

'I don't know,' said Jason. 'But there's something else. We found this in the bag.' He dipped into his pocket and produced a note. Lionel took it and read it. It said,

Received with thanks,
MANUELO

Roger's observatory was in a separate pyramid, a little distance from the first, with tall steep sides and a flat top. There was an open terrace where Roger kept his telescope, and a study for reading and writing. The study was crowded and a little eccentric, with leather chairs, a desk awash with papers, and strange scientific instruments. On a stand in the middle of the floor was a mirror. It caught the rising moonlight through a small square hole in the roof and reflected it around the room like a silver lantern.

On the desk, in the midst of the clutter, stood a blue enamel jar. As Lily sat down, puffed from climbing up the stairs, Roger opened it and held it out to her. The scent of fresh chocolate fudge floated out so strongly that this time Lily knew it was the real thing. She took a piece and popped it into her mouth. Roger took one too, then reached under the desk for a small leather trunk.

'Here you are, Lily Quench.' He removed what looked like a bundle of cloth and dropped it into her arms. Lily caught a heavy shiny object as it slithered out and realised it was her silver helmet, wrapped around by her magical fireproof cape. Then she realised something else. Roger had called her by her real name.

'Your name was embroidered on the cape,' said Roger. He hopped up onto the desk and sat there swinging his legs. 'You're a lucky girl, Lily Quench. If it had been either of the others who found you at the barrier, you wouldn't be standing here now. In fact, you ought to thank me for rescuing you. But we'll let that pass. There are so many other more interesting things to do than make polite conversation.'

'Oh.' Lily felt a rush of anxiety, followed by dozens of questions. Why had Roger brought her here? Where was Queen Dragon? The cry she had heard from the banqueting hall had been so much like hers Lily could not believe she was not somewhere nearby, in terrible danger. To cover her agitation, she shook out her cape and fastened it around her neck. As she did, she saw her name, *Lily Quench*, neatly embroidered in the back of the hood by the weavers of Skellig Lir who had recently repaired it.

'Oh, it's all right,' said Roger, as if he had read her mind. 'I know you don't trust me. Wise, really. I like to think I'm the best of a bad lot, but we magicians are generally a pretty treacherous bunch. Quin and Joscelin are really worried about you, Lily. To tell you the truth, you've got me a little confused, too. It's not every day we get a visit from someone who flies in on a dragon *and* owns a moon rose from the Island of Skellig Lir. Do you want to tell me why you're here?'

Lily hesitated. Despite his friendly manner, she did not precisely trust Roger. 'I'm here because an enemy of my country is using the Eye Stones,' she said guardedly. 'He's planning an invasion out of the past.'

'And because we made the Eye Stones, you came here wanting to find out more about them?' Roger asked. Lily nodded. 'You've done well to track us down, Lily. I suppose they must have told you about us on Skellig Lir.'

'They told me you went to the library there,

45

a long time ago.' Lily thought a moment. 'Hang on. That was ages ago. Centuries. Are you really that old?'

'Ah. That would be telling,' said Roger. 'A magician's got to have some secrets, Lily. Why don't we talk about your quest? You say you want to find out more about the Eye Stones. Are you sure that's all you really want?'

Lily blushed bright red.

'I thought so,' said Roger. 'You want to destroy them, don't you? Well, I can tell you this much. The Eye Stones were built for a purpose. That purpose isn't there anymore, and nowadays the only ones we maintain are the ones in the barrier. I don't think you're really interested in those, are you?'

'No.' It was a relief for Lily to be able to speak frankly. 'Just the ones in the Black Empire, which are within striking distance of Ashby. If I can close the Eye Stones off there, Gordon won't be able to use them to invade us. All I want is to find out where they are, and then I promise Queen Dragon and I will leave.'

'You might have a problem with Joscelin, if you do,' said Roger. 'Queen Dragon's your friend, isn't she? That's quite an achievement, Lily. Joscelin thinks you must be controlling her with some very powerful magic, and he's just dying to know what it is.' He chortled. 'What a joke it would be to tell him the truth.'

'Please don't,' said Lily, in a worried voice.

'Don't worry, I won't,' said Roger. 'But if you take my advice, Lily, you won't linger here. Sooner or later, Joscelin is going to find out what you're really up to, and I wouldn't like to be in your shoes when he does.'

'I'll go when I've finished my quest,' said Lily firmly. 'Do you know where Queen Dragon is?'

'I'm afraid not,' said Roger. 'You see, Joscelin was the one who brought her through the barrier, and much as I'd like to help, I can't afford to get on the wrong side of him. And I can't tell you where to find the Eye Stones, either. Even the ones close to Ashby.'

'Because of Joscelin?'

'No,' said Roger. 'Lily, I'm sorry. The fact is, most of the Eye Stones were only in use for a few hundred years and it's centuries since any of us have even thought about them. If I can't tell you where they are, it's because I can't remember.'

Five

THE PRISONER IN THE PYRAMID

Queen Dragon was a prisoner. She did not know how this had happened, or even when. Her head hurt, she was not thinking logically, and worst of all she did not seem to be able to move. Her wings were spread, her back was arched, and something seemed to have pinned her toes to the ground. It was dimly lit, and she could not see what was happening.

The sound of faraway voices finally penetrated the fog which surrounded her. Queen Dragon could not understand what was being said, but one of the voices sounded familiar. Lily! She seemed to be talking to a man. Queen Dragon's sense of smell was very keen, and she could now smell Lily, clean and fresh as a flower and coming closer. Her excitement grew. *I'm here, Lily! I'm here!*

But her thoughts stayed locked inside her head. Queen Dragon's heart swelled with disappointment as Lily's scent faded, and then all she could smell was the man, his scent mixed in with two other people's. There was something wrong about these scents, something so old and rotten that if Queen Dragon had not been so completely paralysed it would have made her scales stand on end. But the thing that frightened her most was the undernote of blood and death that she scented hanging over all of them. There was something familiar about it that Queen Dragon could not understand. It was not a dragon, but it was definitely dragonish, and it terrified her beyond comprehension.

Wherever she was, Queen Dragon knew Lily was in the most appalling danger…

Lily had finished eating her chocolate fudge. She had looked around Roger's study and been shown outside onto the balustraded terrace where he did his stargazing. In the middle was a square stone table, made from a single chunk of black stone. Lines had been carved on the top; they glowed faintly silver in the dark and marked the points of the compass and other things Lily did not recognise.

'It's a map,' said Roger. 'It shows us where we are in relation to the rest of the world. Come with me, Lily, I want to show you my telescope.' He passed his hand over the table and the writing faded. Lily followed him to the gleaming brass telescope that had been set up on a stone platform at the end of the terrace.

'Why don't we look into your future?' asked Roger slyly. 'I can arrange it, if you would like to.'

'Just at the stars.' Once before, at the ruined

Castle of Mote Ely, someone else had made Lily a similar offer. She had refused it then, and had not changed her mind since.

'As you wish,' said Roger. 'Still, I'd be curious to know what fate has in store for you, Lily Quench.' He looked through the telescope and adjusted a few settings. 'Here. This is Orion: you can see his belt and sword.'

Lily climbed up onto the platform and looked through the eyepiece. 'He looks different where I live,' she said. 'He's lying down, and the sword sticks up like a handle. In Ashby we call him the Saucepan.' It was only in recent times that people in Ashby could see the stars at all. For years, smoke from the Black Count's grommet factory had blotted them out completely. It was a reminder of what might come again if her quest should fail, and Lily felt a little stab of anxiety.

She let Roger show her Jupiter and its moons, then Saturn's rings. 'Mars is my favourite,' he said, 'but he's a bit low down, and it's a bad night for stargazing with the moon so bright. But you'll like this, Lily.' He swung the telescope up so that Lily had to crouch to look through it. 'It looks like a cloud, but it's actually millions of stars. Isn't it marvellous? Doesn't it make you feel like an insignificant grain of dust?'

'I suppose so,' said Lily doubtfully. 'Isn't it all a very long way away?'

'Further than we can even imagine,' Roger assured her. 'It would be a hard thing to travel to the moon, and that's quite close. I've often thought I would like to go there. I would fly through the night on a dragon's wings and make myself king of all I surveyed. I would build a silver tower, the tallest that ever was, and I would live at the very top. No one would be allowed inside except people I invited, and when Joscelin came to visit I would toss him off and let him fall all the way back to earth. What would you do, Lily, if you were Queen of the Moon?'

Lily looked up at its silvery disc. It looked so far-off and desolate it hardly seemed worth being queen of. 'I would plant a garden,' she answered honestly. 'I like plants, and it looks very bare.'

Roger gave a great shout of laughter. '*Touché*, Lily! What an amazing ability you have of putting me back in my place! Well, it's getting cloudy now. I must put away my telescope before it rains.'

He clapped his hands and three pairs of disembodied grey hands appeared and started unscrewing the apparatus. Lily wandered away back towards Roger's study. She paused by the stone tabletop, but all its markings had completely disappeared; if it really was a map, it was a very strange one.

A faint noise from the base of the pyramid distracted her. Lily went to the balustrade and looked over. At the bottom of the pyramid's sloping side a shadowy figure was making its way along the phosphorescent path. A small cart creaked behind it. It was full of scrap metal, ancient gears and flywheels and bits of unidentifiable machinery. A stranger would have thought it was a load of rubbish being taken to the tip under cover of darkness. But Lily, who was intimately acquainted with Queen Dragon, knew immediately what it was.

It was dragon food.

A thrill of fear ran through Lily's body. She had been right all along. The cry she had heard from the banquet hall *had* been a dragon's; a dragon who needed feeding, who must therefore be imprisoned and need her help. Lily glanced furtively around at Roger. He was busy watching his telescope being dismantled and his back was towards her. Lily slipped silently into Roger's study. As she passed his desk she spotted her sword, still in its scabbard, lying under a pile of papers. Lily paused to thrust it into her belt, and ran down the internal stairs to the base of the pyramid.

A little door let her out onto the phosphorescent path. Lily pulled the hood of her cape up over her helmet and set off along the darkened verge. The cart was still squeaking along somewhere ahead, and Lily guessed the person pulling it must be Joscelin. She crept along after him as quietly as she could, keeping a safe distance until she came to a fork in the path. By now the cart had stopped squeaking, and she spent a few moments deciding which way he had gone. At last she decided on the right-hand fork, and after a few minutes' walk came across the cart, abandoned and empty beside the glowing walkway.

It had been pulled up outside yet another pyramid. This one was smaller than both the Great Pyramid and Roger's observatory, but it was still larger than an average size house. A door was open in its side, and two voices were conversing within. Lily listened intently, but the thick stone walls muffled what was being said and she could not identify who was speaking.

After a bit, the talking stopped. A crunching sound started up and this time Lily had no doubt: it *was* a dragon, eating the metal that had been brought on the cart. Lily crept to the open door and tried to peep inside. The interior was too dark for her to see anything, but there was an unmistakable smoky, metallic dragonish scent floating out along the entrance passage. The dragon was eating painfully slowly and breathing heavily between each mouthful. After a while there was a metallic crash, as if some uneaten morsel had fallen to the ground, and a dreadful groaning sound that made Lily's heart turn over.

A human voice spoke. Lily could not make out the words, but before she could creep any closer she saw a light and heard footsteps heading towards her. She took a few steps backward and flung herself down in the grass at the base of the pyramid, just as Joscelin emerged from it. He was carrying something under his cloak, and as he turned towards Lily she caught a glimpse of what looked like a pottery flask with a stopper.

Lily buried her face in the grass and held her breath. All Joscelin had to do was glance down and she would be discovered. But Joscelin was intent on the flask in his hands. Lily heard the gravel crunch under his feet as he stepped back onto the path. He spoke a single word of command to the cart. It trundled of its own accord off the grass onto the gravel and, dismally squeaking, followed him away.

Sighing with relief, Lily sat up. She pushed the hood of her fireproof cape away from her eyes and stood up, brushing off the grass that clung to the front of her clothes. The pyramid door was still open, which made her suspect Joscelin might be coming back, but if it really was Queen Dragon inside the pyramid, she had to find out. Lily crept fearfully forward into the darkness. A few steps along the entrance passage she remembered the little torch she kept in her skirt pocket, took it out, and switched it on.

With every step she took, the scent of dragon grew stronger. Lily heard the rattle of its breath and felt hot smoky air filling her lungs. She coughed, and had to pull her cape around herself to protect her body against the glowing heat. The passage came to an end in front of her. Lily stepped out into a tall chamber and had to clap her hands to her mouth to stop from screaming.

In the middle of the floor, wingless and helpless, lay the chained, sleeping wreck of a dragon.

Six

BABA

It was not Queen Dragon.

Lily's immediate reaction was overwhelming relief. She did not think she could have borne to find her friend in such terrible conditions. The dragon was jammed into a chamber barely big enough to hold it, and was in a most pitiful state. It was thin and obviously sick, and its green scales were coming away in drifts, leaving white, flaky patches of skin along its flanks. Its talons curled around and around, uncut for no one knew how many hundreds of years. But most horrible of all, the dragon's wings had been cut off. All that was left were two tiny stumps of bone and a great long ridge of scar along each flank where the webbing had been hacked away.

Lily felt sick. She knew better than anyone that dragons were dangerous and that they were often the enemies of human beings. But there was also an incredible grandeur about them. This dragon had lost all its magnificence, all its dignity, and Lily judged it could not go on much longer in this state. For while dragons were magical, they were not immortal. They were hard to kill and lived for thousands of years, but they could, and did, eventually die.

'Who are you?'

The voice was little more than a whisper, like a dry leaf rustling on an autumn pavement. Lily started. The dragon had opened its dull eyes and was looking at her. She saw a scale slide down her flank onto the floor, the last of its once vibrant green colour fading as it fell and hit the stone with a tinkle. A host of moulted scales lay around her feet like razor sharp flakes of glass.

Lily took a cautious step forward, aware that a single one could cut her flesh to the bone.

'I—I'm Lily. Lily Quench.'

The dragon sighed. 'I've never seen one as young as you before. Did Joscelin send you?'

'No. I'm here by myself. I'm looking for a friend of mine, another dragon—'

'You're not with Joscelin? You're not…one of them?'

'One of them?' Suddenly Lily realised what the dragon meant. The only human beings she came in contact with here were the magicians. She obviously thought Lily was a magician, too. Lily hastened to explain.

'No,' she said. 'No, I'm not a magician. I came here on a quest with my friend, Queen Dragon. We were separated and I'm trying to find her. Please. Can't you help me track her down?'

'Queen Dragon.' A light suddenly flickered into the dragon's dull eyes. 'You don't mean Sinhault, do you? Sinhault Fierdaze? Oh, my. Oh my, oh my!' The little stumps of wings flapped pitifully at her side. Lily stepped hastily out of the way.

'You know her?'

'Know her? My dear, we were practically

brought up together. I'm Baba, Baba Draco. Sinhault must have mentioned me. Oh, we were such friends in the old days! Tell me, has she met up with the others?'

'The others? Which others?'

'The other dragons, of course.' Baba paused. 'My dear, do you know *anything?*'

'I know what Queen Dragon has told me,' said Lily cautiously. 'I didn't realise there were many other dragons left. Queen Dragon says most of them were wiped out in the Great War of the Dragons, long ago. Her fiancé, King Dragon, went through the Eye Stone in the Black Mountains in the midst of the battle, looking for help. Only he never returned and she has never heard of him since.'

'Sinhault must think that he's lost, then. Well, maybe he is by now.' Baba sighed. 'Sinhault was always crazy about him. That was why we used to call her "Queen Dragon". It was a joke, a nickname. They were going to be married, but then the Great War came. We went through the Eye Stone, but King Dragon said Sinhault was too young, that she had to hide and wait among the rocks until he came back.'

'Hold on,' said Lily. 'There's something I don't think I'm following here. Are you saying that *you* went through the Eye Stone with King Dragon? That King Dragon might still be alive somewhere?'

'As far as I know, he could be,' said Baba. 'Yes, I was with him. There were seven of us. King Dragon, Kniphofia Scarlet, Petrified Snaketongue and his girlfriend Scaletooth, my sister Annacondia and myself. The last dragon was someone I didn't know very well. He was called Balefire, but he was badly injured as he went through the Eye Stone and he—died. That was where all our problems started. Or mine did, at any rate.'

'Do you mean problems with the magicians?' asked Lily.

'In a manner of speaking,' said Baba bitterly. 'It's a long story, Lily. Even if I had the strength to do it, I do not think I could bear to tell you the whole. You see, dragons are naturally magical creatures. That makes us useful to magicians for all sorts of reasons, alive or dead. For years, Joscelin and his friends used to hunt dragons down. They built those Eye Stone things in places that dragons used to frequent, and they would come through and ambush them, kill them, even take them captive.

'At last, Joscelin came up with a plan that would give him more dragons than even he could need. He planted a magical statue on the cliff at Dragon's Downfall and lured the dragons into starting the war. The war gave him dead dragons—lots of them. Then he tricked the seven of us into going through the Eye Stone. His plan was to take all of us prisoner, but the others escaped.'

'That's *horrible*,' said Lily. A great sense of indignation and distress welled up inside her. 'How can Joscelin have left you here all this time? Are the magicians…are they actually human?'

'Personally, I think it's debatable,' said Baba. 'I suppose they were, once. Their long life is artificial, of course. Only dragons live so long. But every night the magicians drink a magic potion. It's laced with a few drops of my blood, and that gives them access to a little of my longevity. Joscelin makes it, and only he knows the recipe. That is why he is able to control the other two. They're scared of him, even Roger. All he has to do is refuse to give them the potion, and they will grow old and die very quickly.'

Lily was aghast. 'They drink a potion with your *blood* in it? But…but dragons' blood—'

'Burns? Yes, I know,' said Baba. 'I'd say their spells have burned away pretty nearly everything that was human about them. Oh, there might be a little kernel left, the bit that even their spells can't touch, but by now that must be so deeply hidden I doubt they even realise it exists.'

Lily remembered the moment, not so very long ago, when she had accidentally been splashed with Queen Dragon's blood on the ramparts of Mote Ely Castle. She could not begin to imagine what it would be like to drink even a few drops mixed with other ingredients. And she could not imagine what it was like for Baba, having lost her wings, her freedom, and the companionship of her own kind; being reduced to a supply of spare parts for the magicians' evil purposes.

'How long has this been going on?' she asked.

'I don't know,' said Baba in a tired voice. 'I can't remember. Three thousand years maybe. I don't like to count anymore. In the beginning, I thought that the others would come back and rescue me. But they never did and I realise now they never will. You see, I let them down. If Sinhault ever hears the whole story, I'm sure she will abandon me too.'

'Never,' said Lily firmly. 'Queen Dragon's not like that. I'm sure she will forgive you, whatever you did. And I know she will want to speak to you, if only I can find her. She's longed to discover what has happened to King Dragon for thousands of years. Even if he's dead, she would want to find out.'

'I can't tell you where she is,' said Baba, 'but they will be holding her prisoner somewhere. My guess is that they've put her in one of the other pyramids. There are dozens of them, dotted about, but you'll need to be careful, Lily. I'm not the only magical creature locked up here, and some of the others are not as friendly as I am.'

'I'll go and search straightaway,' promised Lily, 'and when I find her we'll come back and rescue you.'

Baba smiled faintly. 'I'm past rescuing, Lily. Just find Sinhault and set her free. It's important. You see, for centuries the magicians have done everything they can to keep me alive. You'd be amazed how many spells use bits of dragon. Scales, teeth. I haven't many of those left now. And blood, of course. But my blood isn't what it used to be: they know I'm dying. And when I die, so do they—unless they can find a healthy dragon as a replacement.' She paused meaningfully. 'I think you can imagine the rest, Lily. There aren't very many dragons around nowadays. Find Sinhault and get away from this evil place as quickly as you can.'

'We will,' Lily promised. 'But not until we've finished our quest. Perhaps you can help—'

She broke off as a weird silver light flooded the passage behind her.

'It's Joscelin!' hissed Baba. 'He's come back. Quick, Lily! Hide!'

Seven

AMONG THE PYRAMIDS

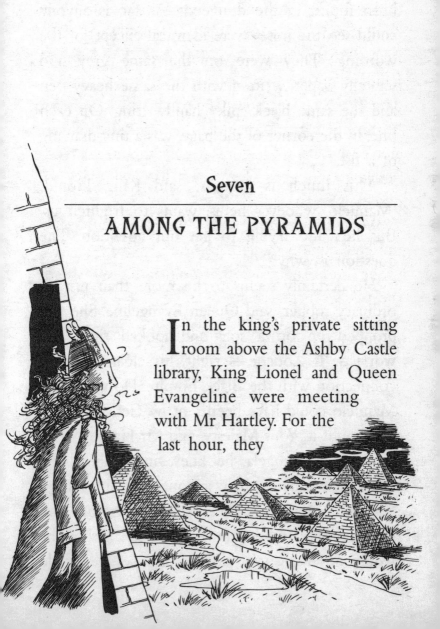

In the king's private sitting room above the Ashby Castle library, King Lionel and Queen Evangeline were meeting with Mr Hartley. For the last hour, they had been poring over the two messages that had been found in the dungeons. As far as anyone could see, the notes were identical except for the wording. They were on the same grey and scratchy paper, written with the same heavy pen and the same black spiky handwriting. On each one, in the corner of the page, was a tiny drawing of a fist.

'This much is certain,' said King Lionel. 'Manuelo, whoever he is, wants to frighten us. But he's also trying to get our attention. The question is, why?'

'He certainly seems to be more than just an ordinary robber,' said Queen Evangeline. She was propped up on a sofa and looked tired and worried. 'If Zouche is right, his cloak means a connection with the Black Empire. Do you think Manuelo could have been sent by General Sark?'

'I doubt it, Your Majesty,' said Mr Hartley. With his wife, Dr Angela, he knew more about the Black Mountains than anyone else in Ashby. 'General Sark is a soldier. He is treacherous, but not cunning. If he planned to attack Ashby, he would never give you advance notice. He would simply send in his troops and tanks and overrun you.'

'The note couldn't have been sent by Sark for another reason, too, Evie,' said Lionel. 'Why would Sark steal one bag of gold from the Treasure of Mote Ely? He rules the Black Empire, he already has a fortune at his disposal. Manuelo has to be someone else. And I'm afraid I think I know who he might be.'

A name hung, unspoken, in the air. Queen Evangeline looked at Mr Hartley, and Mr Hartley looked at Lionel. At last, Evangeline cleared her throat and spoke.

'You mean Gordon?'

'I'm afraid so,' said Lionel. 'The letter is signed Manuelo, but if Gordon is working in secret, he might want to conceal his identity. There's another reason why I think it's Gordon, too. When I helped him at Mote Ely Castle, he promised that in return he would give me fair warning before invading Ashby. We know Gordon has been planning to come back from the past with an army. Ever since we met him at Mote Ely, Lily and Queen Dragon have been working to find the Eye Stones and close them off, to stop him doing just that. Well, perhaps this is the warning Gordon promised me. Perhaps he's already arrived.'

'You mean, he's here in our time?' Evangeline's eyes were wide with alarm. 'With an army?'

Mr Hartley shook his head. 'If an army had invaded the Black Mountains, I am sure we would have heard,' he said. 'Remember, Angela was a slave in the Black Mountains. She still has many friends in the mining camps and the Black Citadel, and we both keep our ears to the ground. An army is a very big thing, Your Majesty. It would not arrive unseen. Besides, it is getting close to winter now and in a few weeks the Black Mountains will be completely snowed in. Gordon will know that. He grew up there. In winter it will be impossible to move large numbers of troops around or even to feed them. I cannot believe Gordon would be silly enough to take an army to the Black Mountains now.'

'But Ashby's winters are mild,' said Evangeline fearfully. 'It never snows here. Suppose Gordon decides to attack Ashby first and then go to the Black Mountains?'

'He might, Evie,' said Lionel. 'But I doubt it

very much. Gordon's birthright is the Black Empire. Ashby was a tiny part of that for about ten years. I know that he will try to reclaim it, but he will want the Black Citadel first. His first target will be General Sark. These attacks may be the beginning, but I think we still have a little time.'

'Then why leave these notes?' demanded Evangeline.

'I don't know,' admitted Lionel. 'That's the problem.'

'If I may just say something, Your Majesty,' said Mr Hartley, 'I think we are fighting against more than Gordon and his army here. The Black Empire was always a home to evil. It was built on blood and fear and death over hundreds of years by a long line of depraved and selfish men. And even before that, the Black Mountains were always a bad place. Think of the Great War of the Dragons, of the magical statue of the Golden Child that Lily and Queen Dragon destroyed at Dragon's Downfall. Gordon is an ordinary boy, but all this is in his bloodline. If he tries to lay hold of that inheritance it will ultimately claim him, just as it did his father and all the Black

Counts before him. The only chance for him to escape that is to fail in his attempt to regain his father's empire.'

'You mean,' said Lionel, 'that Gordon gave us warning because he *wants* us to succeed?'

'At some level, I think he does,' said Mr Hartley. 'You see, Your Majesty, compared to his forebears, Gordon is lucky. He had Angela as his foster-mother and he has spent time with Lily and Queen Dragon. He has seen the other side of the coin, and it does not have his father's picture on it. But whenever he tries to look for a way out, there are forces blocking his way he can't withstand by his own strength. That is why I say we are fighting more than simply Gordon. We are in a battle against the powers of evil that lie behind his heritage.'

'That sounds hopeless,' said Evangeline, dismayed. 'How can we possibly stand against that? We might as well give up now.'

'Not at all,' said Mr Hartley, in a reassuring voice. 'In my experience, the powers of evil have only a very limited range of tricks. When once you learn them, they are very easy to recognise. The first one is deception—lies and trickeries.

If this fails, they will try to distract you from your purpose. When you withstand that, they will frighten you and discourage you, and finally, they will try to attack you. But remember, it is always largely bluff. They have no real power over you. You are the one who has power over them—as long as you have faith and stand firm.'

'One thing is certain,' said Lionel. 'With Gordon threatening like this, it is more important than ever that Lily and Queen Dragon should find out where those Eye Stones are and close them off.'

'Lily is a Quench,' said Mr Hartley. 'The Quenches have always been great fighters. And her mother was a Cornstalk, and Cornstalks love peace. Lily has eyes in her head, and in her heart as well. I am praying for her protection, and I am not afraid for her.'

'I've just had an idea!' exclaimed Queen Evangeline. 'Those two boys, Tom and Murdo, the ones we rescued in the past at Mote Ely Castle. They were in Gordon's army. We could ask them if Gordon ever used the name Manuelo!'

'And I have several notebooks from the time I

spent in the Black Mountains,' said Mr Hartley. 'I'll reread them tonight and see if Manuelo is mentioned.'

'I will go and search the Royal Library,' said King Lionel. He was never happier than when he was messing around among his books. 'There must be a clue to this mystery, somewhere. Whoever he is, Manuelo will be found and dealt with!'

In the shadows behind Baba's enormous foreleg, Lily crouched and pulled her hood down over her eyes. The light in the corridor was coming closer. A figure in a dark cloak entered the chamber. Lily stole a furtive glance around Baba's leg and saw that it wasn't Joscelin after all.

It was Roger.

'Good evening, Baba,' Roger said. 'Is anything amiss? I was surprised to find the door open. I suppose you're hardly in any condition to leave, but it's unlike Joscelin to be so careless.' Baba shrugged, and he went on, 'Not saying anything, dearheart? I thought I heard voices in here. I was looking for a visitor of ours who's lost. A girl with a silver helmet and fair hair, about so high. I don't suppose she's been here?'

Lily felt a shudder ripple through Baba's body. Her scales lifted slightly, as Queen Dragon's did when she was alarmed or frightened. One loosened, razor sharp platelet suddenly stood out on end next to Lily's face and she ducked just in time to avoid being slashed by it. Lily grabbed the scale and pushed it down with all her strength until it sat flush against Baba's side.

'Or perhaps you were talking to yourself,' said Roger, as a familiar squeaking sounded in the entrance to the pyramid. 'Never mind. Here's Joscelin coming to drench you. That will give you something to take your mind off things, won't it?'

'What are you doing here?' A harsh voice spoke unexpectedly loudly. Lily jumped. For a terrifying instant, she thought she had been discovered. Then she realised that Joscelin was talking to Roger. She peeped over Baba's leg and saw him standing with the wheeled cart he had been using earlier in the evening. It was now loaded down with a horrible contraption that looked like a giant syringe hooked up to a metal tank.

Roger bowed politely. 'Just looking in on our dragon friend,' he said, sounding normal and cheerful. 'You left the door open, Joscelin. I was concerned something might have happened.'

'I've been fetching my drenching equipment,' said Joscelin. 'What are you doing in this pyramid? You know it's out of bounds to you.'

'I was just on the way back to my observatory,' said Roger. 'I've been having a little talk with Lily.'

'Now that we have captured the dragon, Lily is not important,' said Joscelin. 'Let Quin deal with her from now on. She wastes less time and is less given to sentiment than you are.'

'As you wish, Joscelin.' Roger bowed again. He backed away towards the entrance, turned on his heel, and was gone.

Joscelin waited until his footsteps faded and turned to Baba. For a long while, maybe half a minute, he stood looking her over, measuring her up. A feeling of intense danger ran down Lily's arm and she felt another shudder of fear ripple through Baba's body. Joscelin's inspection finished.

Lily saw him unhook a stepladder from a nearby wall and set it up close to Baba's face. She heard the soft rattle of a hose unwinding. A moment later Baba recoiled sharply and started squealing in pain and terror.

Lily yelled out too. In any other circumstance, her cry of fright would have immediately given her away, but the noise Baba was making was so horrendous it would have drowned out an army of elephants. Lily had never heard anything like it in her life. It was shrill, agonised and inhuman, a convulsed scream that almost made the pyramid shake, it was so loud and desperate. Lily clapped her hands over her ears, but it was useless. Then, as Baba twisted and writhed, her right foreleg suddenly shifted, trapping Lily between her leg and body.

'Help!' Two monumental walls of dragon flesh and scale closed in and started slowly crushing her. Lily's eyes bulged in her head. She felt the breath squeeze from her lungs; only her fireproof cape protected her from being burned from head to foot by Baba's scales. Lily saw something swing towards her face and ducked instinctively. The razor sharp scale she had already pushed back into place had flipped up again and grazed within a hairsbreadth of her cheek.

'*Ow!*' Any closer, and the scale would have ripped the side of her face off. Lily punched at it, but her arm was trapped and she couldn't get enough swing to knock it away. The scale flapped back and forth, dangerously close to her head. Then the hood of Lily's fireproof cape flopped down over her eyes and she could not see at all.

It was as if she was trapped in a sack, being squashed between two millstones, with an axe being swung at her head. Lily screamed for help, no longer caring who heard. Then suddenly her left arm, the arm with the scales on it, wriggled free. It thrust out of her fireproof cape, slid, scale against scale, over Baba's burning body, and punched upward with a life of its own.

With a *thwock!* the deadly scale ripped out of Baba's flank and hit the wall, falling in tinkling shards onto the floor. And at that exact moment, Baba's burning flesh went deathly cold. Her fires went out. She stopped writhing, stopped screaming, and slumped unconscious on the floor with a hideous thud.

If Baba's falling body had landed slightly to the

right, Lily would have been squashed to a grease spot. Instead, the dragon fell straight where she was standing. Lily went down with her. She lay trapped behind Baba's massive foreleg, unable to move an inch. Lily heard Joscelin's cart being wheeled down the passage to the entrance and the light went out.

'Baba? Baba! Can you hear me? I'm stuck! I'm trapped! Please, wake up!'

Baba stirred and groaned. She lifted her head slightly and dropped it back down on her forelegs. A small gap opened up and Lily scrambled out, shaking and breathless. Baba was lying slumped on the pyramid floor, her green colour faded to a sickly chartreuse. There were tears in her eyes and thick mucus dribbled from her nostrils. It was an unnatural, sulphury yellow colour, and it rattled in her sinuses when she tried to speak.

'I'm sorry, Lily,' she said weakly. 'Joscelin does that once a week. He puts some potion in the syringe and injects it up my nostrils. It puts out my fires so I can't attack him. It always makes me *so* ill.'

'I'm sorry, Baba.' Lily laid her hand briefly on

Baba's foot. It felt dangerously cold and she found herself wondering how long she could last like this. Baba leaned forward and spoke to her urgently, in a voice that was little more than a forced whisper.

'You must go quickly now, Lily. You heard what Joscelin said. Sinhault has been captured, she is in terrible peril. Find her and rescue her, and then both of you leave the pyramids as quickly as you can. There is nothing in this place for dragons except death!'

The path outside was deserted, the night was cool. A little wind soughed through the tussocky grass, but the moon had gone behind a cloud. At the door of Baba's pyramid, Lily paused a moment to look out across the landscape. Somewhere out in the darkness, in one of the pyramids whose angular shapes dotted the night, Queen Dragon lay imprisoned.

There were probably twenty pyramids in all. Lily could hardly bear to think where Queen Dragon might be, or what might be happening to her; nor had she any real idea how she might rescue her. But despite Joscelin and his knowledge of dragons, despite Quin and Roger and the magical barrier of Eye Stones protecting their territory, she had to prevail. Even if they had made a horrible mistake in coming here and their quest to discover the Eye Stones' whereabouts failed utterly, Lily knew she could never live with the thought of abandoning her friend.

She set out across the grass towards the next pyramid. It was rough going in the darkness, and once or twice she stepped in little streams that wet her boots and soaked her socks. The pyramid stood open to the air and contained nothing but dust and rubble; and a second was also disused. But the third pyramid Lily came to was different. Its entrance was overgrown with weeds and inside were racks of stone sarcophagi, stacked like wine bottles in a cellar.

It was a creepy sight. In her pre-quenching days, Lily would have screamed; as it was, the Cornstalk half of her heart beat fast at the sight. Several of the sarcophagi had cracked or broken lids, and Lily forced herself to look inside one. There was no body or mummy inside, but the bottom was covered with a sludgy, smelly liquid and a nest of centipedes swarmed out at her approach and slithered away into the darkest recesses of the chamber. Lily clapped her hands over her face. She had seen enough. There was no way Queen Dragon could be hidden here.

Then she heard something. It was the sound of an animal growling softly in the furthest corner of the pyramid. For a fraction of a second, Lily hesitated, torn between the thought of Queen Dragon imprisoned, and the memory of Baba's warning about dangerous creatures hidden in the pyramids. Very carefully, keeping her back to the stack of sarcophagi, she started inching towards the noise.

Her torch beam passed over walls covered with panels of strange spiky writing. There were no doors, nor any sign that any person or creature had passed this way before her. Lily swung her light into the corner where the noise was coming from. The growling noise rose in anger and intensity as she approached, and Lily unexpectedly found herself at a dead end, facing into the dusty corner of the pyramid and staring at an incredible painting.

It was a picture of a creature like a lion, painted on the plaster when it was still wet. It was so big, Lily guessed it must be life-size, though she had never seen such an animal in real life. Underneath the flaking paint, Lily noticed that its flanks were striped and that its tail had a barb like a dragon's, covered with eyes. Its teeth overhung its jaw like a walrus's tusks and its white front was streaked with what looked like blood. One dark eye was turned towards her and seemed to glitter with a terrible malevolence.

Lily stepped forward for a closer look. She had hardly shone her torch in the creature's face when it roared, turned its head, and thrust its slavering jaws out of the wall straight at her.

Eight

THE FIREBALL

Lily screamed. The lion creature's head thrust forward, plunging towards her, spraying saliva and flooding her face with its hot, stinking breath. A huge claw snagged her skirt and ripped it to the hem. Lily stumbled backwards. Her left foot doubled over and she fell, banging her head so hard against a sarcophagus that it jarred her teeth and sent her sprawling to the floor.

Pink dots buzzed in front of Lily's eyes. Her head reeled as she tried to get up. Snarling and snapping, the lion creature struggled to get out of the wall. Yet something kept jerking it back, stopping its teeth from sinking into her flesh. Lily fumbled for her dropped torch. As its dim light flickered over the lion, she saw that its head, body and front legs were out of the picture. Only its back legs had failed to come to life with the rest of it. Bits of plaster had fallen away from the wall and the paint had faded. Its hindquarters were trapped in the wall and almost eroded away by age and damp.

As Lily watched, the creature blinked, shrank down on itself, and went back into the wall. Just in time, she snapped out her torch. A light had appeared at the pyramid's entrance.

She was trapped in the furthest corner of the pyramid. Helplessly, Lily looked around for somewhere to hide. The nearest sarcophagi all had lids, but there was a gap between two coffins on the bottom of the stack. With nothing to lose, Lily dived into the space and squirmed away like a worm in the darkness. It was dark and dank there, and the space was so small that a less desperate person would have called it impossible. But Lily *was* desperate. As the footsteps came nearer she wriggled around a corner. The space she was in suddenly widened, and she found herself in an unexpected hiding place, an unseen cavity between the front and back ranks of stacked stone coffins.

Lily lay as still and quiet as a corpse. She felt like a fossil trapped in a rock, with thousands of tonnes of granite stacked precariously like the centuries over her head. Her nose filled with the musty, decayed scent of the sarcophagi. Something wriggled over her face and she bit her lip to stop from screaming.

Her heart was pounding so hard it seemed it must give her away. But no one came. No one called her. There was nothing to be heard but the sound of unseen rustlings in the darkness.

At last, Lily could bear her dark imprisonment no longer. Getting out was more difficult than getting in, but she managed at last to turn around and wriggle back out. As she emerged from the stack of coffins, a bright pale light flared up in front of her.

'Hello, Lily,' said a voice.

Still on her hands and knees, Lily looked up. It was Quin. A small white ball of fire hovered next to her head. In its stark white light her face was like a piece of marble, her plaits like a nest of snakes on the back of her head. Her dark eyes glittered, and as they locked with Lily's, a bolt of pain like lightning exploded along Lily's arm...

In the Ashby Hospital, the nurses were doing their evening rounds. Dr Angela Hartley was about to go home. She had been working late, delivering a baby that had decided to come into the world a whole month before its mother had expected it. Dr Angela had just written AMY JANE PONSONBY on the baby's impressive parchment birth certificate when a tap sounded on the glass door of her office. It was Queen Evangeline of Ashby, rugged up against the evening cool in a fancy knitted jumper and black ski pants.

Dr Angela rolled up Amy Jane's birth certificate and popped it in a tray for the nurse to collect later. She hurried over to let the queen in.

'Your Majesty! Is something the matter?'

'Don't worry, there's no emergency.' Evangeline glanced down at her pregnant tummy. 'I was wondering if I could speak with one of your patients. It's Murdo, the boy from Mote Ely, the one who broke his legs when he was pushed down the well.'

'Of course,' said Angela. 'Murdo's not doing too badly. He'll be out of plaster soon and he's walking quite well on crutches. But he's not very communicative, Your Majesty. You might be better off speaking to the other lad, Tom, who came with him. He's living with the head gardener and his wife at the botanic gardens.'

'I've just spoken to Tom,' said Evangeline. 'He's settling in well, but he couldn't help me. Murdo is my last chance, Angela. If he's well enough to talk, I'd like to see him tonight.'

'Then I'll take you to him straightaway,' said Angela, opening the door to her office. 'But I can't promise he'll be helpful. Last week we had to take Murdo out of the children's ward and put him in a room by himself. He was threatening to hit the other children with his crutches. They were scared of him, and their parents…well, complained.'

'I don't blame them,' said Evangeline. 'Oh dear. This doesn't sound very promising.'

'It's hardly surprising,' said Angela. 'I imagine he's terrified. Look at it from his point of view. When Murdo was pushed down the well in Mote Ely Castle, he was knocked unconscious. When he woke up, he found himself two hundred years in the future. Everything here is so different to what he's used to. He doesn't understand electric light or air-conditioning, or half the things the doctors and nurses here have done to him. No wonder he doesn't trust us. All he knows is that we are Lily's friends—and that Lily was his general's, Gordon's, enemy.'

'The Librarian at Skellig Lir told Lily it was perilous to travel into the future,' said Evangeline. 'I wish we'd known that before we brought Murdo into our time.'

'If we'd left Murdo in the past, he would have died,' said Angela firmly. 'It can't be wrong to save someone's life. This is his room here, Your Majesty.' She tapped on a door and a voice called out for them to come in. 'Good evening, nurse. Hello, Murdo, how are you feeling?'

Evangeline followed Angela into the room. A boy was sitting up in bed, wearing a blue hospital nightshirt. Both his legs were in plaster and there was a scar over his left temple which had not quite healed. His face was plain, freckled, pinched and suspicious. When he saw Evangeline, a sudden change came over it and he flinched with fear.

'Doctor Hartley,' said the nurse, 'could you persuade Murdo to take his medicine? I've told him it will ease the pain and help him sleep, but he won't listen to a word I say.'

'Murdo has terrible nightmares,' explained Angela. 'When he was in the ward, he often woke the other children with his screaming.' She went over and started looking at his head, but Murdo snarled and twisted away from her.

Evangeline pulled up a chair and sat down beside the bed. 'Poor Murdo,' she said sympathetically. 'You must have had an awful time. Do you remember me?'

'You're the queen,' said Murdo sullenly. 'The

general told me about you. He said you were a traitor to his father and the Black Empire.'

It was not an answer Evangeline had expected, and she flushed bright crimson. In the past her family, the Brights, had been among the Black Count's keenest supporters in Ashby. She herself had been on the board of the Count's Ashby Water grommet factory, and her mother, Crystal, still complained that life had never been so bad since the Black Squads left. But Evangeline believed she had moved on to better things. She also knew that most people thought her a nicer person for the changes that had taken place in her life. To be reminded of her past was disconcerting and not very nice.

'It's all a matter of how you look at it, isn't it?' she said. 'I suppose by "the general" you mean Gordon?' Murdo did not reply, and Evangeline pressed on, 'You must have been fond of him to feel this way.'

'The general was all right,' said Murdo. 'At least he let me and my sister, Veronica, stay together. And Rabbit too, worse luck,' he added under his breath, and Evangeline remembered that it had been Murdo's brother, Rabbit, who had pushed him down the well. 'The general let me be an officer and dig for treasure in the castle cellars. I would have found it, too, if it wasn't for Rabbit.'

'I'm sure you would have,' said Evangeline uneasily. The fact that the treasure Murdo had pinned his hopes on finding was the real reason for her visit, was something she thought it better to keep to herself. 'Tell me, Murdo. Would you like to see the general again?'

Murdo's reaction was swift and frightening. A thin hand shot out and grabbed Evangeline's arm, the fingers boring into her flesh. 'Do you mean it?' he demanded hoarsely. 'Would you send me back there? Back to the castle, back to Veronica?'

'I wasn't talking about sending you back, exactly,' Evangeline floundered. Murdo's face was filled with such desperate longing she could hardly bear to look at it. She knew there was no way Lionel would send Murdo back when Gordon was threatening an invasion. 'Actually, I was wondering if you could tell me something about Manuelo.'

Murdo let go of her arm. His already pale skin went even whiter and there was a strange expression on his face that was partly hope, partly dread. For a moment his lips parted and Evangeline thought he was about to say something. She looked at him eagerly, waiting for him to reply.

'I don't know who you're talking about,' Murdo said. And with that, he sank back on the pillows, turned his face to the wall beside the bed and refused to say any more.

'Stand up, Lily,' said Quin.

Lily crouched on the floor in front of her. Her teeth chattered in her head. A fear more dreadful than anything she had experienced since her earliest days as a Quencher had engulfed her. She wanted to run away, but she could not believe that if she tried she would succeed. The pain in her arm, normally a warning, was this time so bad it almost paralysed her. She could not have disobeyed Quin, even if she had wanted to.

Lily stood up slowly. Her head was so confused by pain and terror, and the light from Quin's fireball dazzled her eyes. For some reason, all she could think of was the gold dress Quin had laid out for her in the pyramid. It glittered like a mirage in the desert before her open eyes; it danced inside her head when she closed them. Lily started walking towards it. It was so beautiful she could not understand why she had resisted wearing it. It had puffed sleeves, and its silk petticoat was embroidered with roses and daisies, like her name. Daisy. Her name was Daisy Rose, and she was Quin's dearest, only daughter. She loved her mother so much there was nothing she wouldn't do to please her. Nothing else she could do with such a beautiful present as this, except put it on.

She picked up the dress and held it to her cheek. It was soft, so soft. There were tiny pintucks sewn all over the bodice, and pearls on the neckline. Daisy Rose. She had to please her mother.

Except, her mother was dead.

The thought came like an arrow out of nowhere and struck deep in her heart. Her mother. She was a picture in a black and white photograph, a bride in a white dress with a huge bouquet of flowers... Daisy. Daisy. Daisy Rose.

The picture grew larger and larger. The bouquet grew bigger and bigger and suddenly a small chink opened up in the cloud of confusion that surrounded her. *Who are you?* said a voice inside her head, and in answer the photograph of the bride burst forth like a sunrise in brilliant colour, and the flowers in the bouquet were neither daisies nor roses but glorious pink and white lilies.

Lily. She was Lily Quench.

The terror still gripped her, but now Lily could resist it. The muddling sense of fear was coming from Quin, pouring out of her like a thick cloud of choking smoke. Fixing her thoughts on her mother's photo, Lily started walking towards her. Quin smiled, as if this was what she had been expecting her to do. Lily walked a little faster, then suddenly broke into a run. At the last moment, as she dashed past, she threw up both her hands and shoved Quin as hard as she could in the stomach.

Quin gave a shocked cry and stumbled, the heel of one of her high shoes catching in her dress and pitching her backwards into one of the coffins. Lily did not wait to see what happened next. As she darted out through the door she felt suddenly, gloriously free, and, though her heart still pounded with fear and excitement, she realised that, whatever it had been, Quin's magical hold over her had failed.

'Come back!' Lily heard Quin shouting. *'Come back!'* Lily glanced over her shoulder. Quin had emerged from the pyramid and was standing by the side of the path, unable to run in her high shoes. For a moment, Lily thought she was actually going to make it—and then suddenly something zipped past her ear.

It was a ball of light, bright white and tinged with blue. Lily cried out, stumbled, and almost fell. The fireball whisked in front of her face like an insect, the light stabbing at her eyes until she was almost blinded. It pushed her back, turning her aside and heading her off the grass. The fireball was chasing her away from the darkness towards the glowing path, and nothing she could do would make it go away.

In the open space before the main pyramid, Lily at last hit the path again. She made one last attempt to swat the fireball. Her fingers grazed against it and she yelped, for it was so cold it burned. Glowing stones scattered like chips of fire under her boots, and she skidded and began to fall. But Lily never hit the ground. She had a brief glimpse of Quin behind her, surfing over the ground on a disc of blue light, and then she went flying up through the air, out of control and turning somersaults until she was giddy and about to throw up. She saw the pyramids below her, far more of them than she had realised. Then she saw the main pyramid with its gaping entrance, the eye on the lintel watching, waiting. A dark vortex opened up within it, and Lily realised that it was another Eye Stone, like the ones at Dragon's Downfall, on Skansey, at Mote Ely. Unable to stop herself, Lily flew towards it and it sucked her in, spinning her around like a leaf in a whirlpool. A crushing weight bore down on her. She felt her body squeeze in on itself, and then suddenly she shot out of the eye, hit something hard and stuck.

'Help!' Lily's cry got no further than the thought. Her throat was frozen, she could not speak. Strange shapes sparkled in front of her eyes, fantastic yet familiar: unicorns and manticores, hippogriffs and centaurs, minotaurs and phoenixes

and salamanders. She had seen the same creatures only a few hours ago, on the ceiling of the magicians' banqueting hall. They seemed brighter and more real this time, and the rest of the room had gone dim. There was something else that was different too, though she could not at first work out what it was. Then Lily realised. She was not looking up, she was looking down. And the creatures were looking down too. It was at that moment that she realised the awful truth. She was Lily no longer, but only a picture, flat and lifeless and unable to move. She was stuck in the banqueting hall ceiling, and Queen Dragon's despairing eyes were looking across at her from the other side of the room.

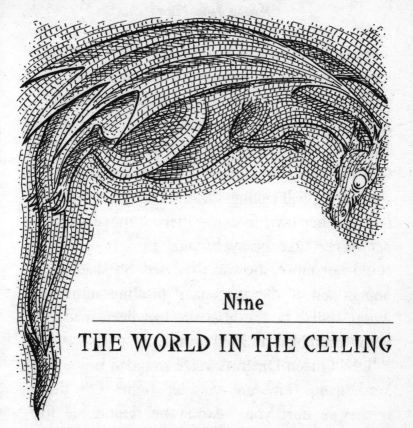

Nine

THE WORLD IN THE CEILING

'Lily. Lily, can you hear me?' A familiar voice sounded inside Lily's head. It did not seem to be coming from anywhere in particular. Lily looked at Queen Dragon, but her mouth was not moving and neither was her head. Queen Dragon almost always waggled her head when she talked. But then, like Lily herself, Queen Dragon was not exactly her normal self.

She looked very big and very clear, her body surrounded by a sunburst of gold mosaic. The image had been perfectly rendered, as if a master-artist had worked her portrait in chips of glass. Only this was no portrait. This was the real Queen Dragon, magically trapped in the banqueting hall ceiling. On the edge of her vision Lily saw her own feet in glittering mosaic boots, her fingers like glassy bananas in a bunch. She could not move, she was paralysed. She had been imprisoned at the magicians' pleasure until the world ended, or the glass she had been made of failed, crumbled and fell away.

'Lily.' Queen Dragon's voice sounded inside her head again. 'Lily, are you all right? Oh dear. If they've hurt you I won't be responsible for what I do!'

Instinctively, Lily turned her reply into a thought and flung it back at her. 'I'm here, Queen Dragon!'

'*Ouch!*' screeched a stranger's voice inside her head. 'There's no need to shout, you know. Some of us are trying to sleep!'

'I'm sorry!' Lily had flung the thought out as far and as hard as she could; it had not occurred to her that anyone else might hear. 'I'm very new to this. I didn't realise I was shouting!'

'Then learn fast,' snapped the voice, 'and it will be more pleasant for all of us.' What sounded suspiciously like a raspberry rang out in Lily's head, and then was silent.

'Don't mind him, Lily,' said Queen Dragon. 'He's a bit bad tempered. He doesn't like the fact that I'm here. A royal dragon is bound to make a mere griffin look small,' she added, loudly enough that the griffin, whom Lily now saw beside Queen Dragon, was bound to hear. 'Are you hurt, Lily? You arrived with a bit of a bang, you know. The rest of us got an awful shock.'

'The rest of us? You mean, the other creatures in the ceiling?' Lily looked again at the griffin, at two unicorns, a hippogriff, and a golden phoenix. They too, were alive, just like Queen Dragon and herself. Lily became aware that there were all sorts of conversations going on around them. The unicorns were singing, and a manticore was growling at a tiger with two tails. There were other creatures too, some of whom she could hear, but glimpse only imperfectly from her position at the end of the room. It was a bit like being at a party with several conversations going on at once.

'Don't mind them,' said Queen Dragon. 'They lost interest in you as soon as they realised you were a human. The phoenix was a bit sniffy at first, because he thought you lowered the tone of the place, but the rest couldn't care less. Some of the creatures have been here a very long time, Lily. Thousands of years in some cases. It seems to make them either mad or rather narrow-minded.'

'That's understandable,' said Lily faintly. It crossed her mind to wonder what she would be like herself when she had been a picture for two thousand years, but the thought was so awful she pushed it away. 'What are they here for?'

'I believe they're hunting trophies,' said Queen Dragon. 'That Quin woman does experiments on them, or uses bits of them for spells. The one who's interested in me is Joscelin. He claims to be an expert on dragons.' She snorted scornfully. 'It's debatable, if you ask me. Your old ancestor Matilda Quench could have taught him a thing or two, and you know my opinion of *her*.'

Since Matilda Quench had killed Queen

Dragon's friend, Serpentine Bridgestock, and was something of a sore point between them, Lily thought it best not to pick up on this. 'Was Joscelin the one who caught you?'

If she had not been a mosaic, Queen Dragon would probably have blushed. 'It was my own fault,' she admitted. 'After you disappeared I let him lure me through the barrier. I know it was very silly of me, but I was so anxious, I couldn't help myself.'

'I was silly, too,' said Lily glumly, and she recounted her adventures since her capture. Talking with her thoughts reminded her of her attempts to speak with the telepathic sea dragons on the island of Skellig Mor. This was far easier, for in a half-world where everyone was flat, telepathy was the natural method of communication. Unfortunately, it also made it difficult to hide things. Lily had hoped to soften the bad news about Baba, but the experience was so vividly recent in her memory that her thoughts ran away with her and she found herself revealing far more than she had intended.

'So Baba is alive,' Queen Dragon whispered. 'And the other dragons…'

'Baba couldn't tell me whether they were still alive, Queen Dragon,' said Lily. 'It's thousands of years since they left her. Please. Don't get your hopes up.'

'But King Dragon survived!' If she had not been a mosaic, Queen Dragon would have been thrashing about in distress. 'He survived the Great War of the Dragons! He may be alive to this day, Lily! Where is he now? Why did he never come for me? I have to speak to Baba. I have to! I must find out what's happened!'

'We'll find out, Queen Dragon. I promise you, we'll find out.' Was it Lily's imagination, or was the mosaic around Queen Dragon's eyes glistening more brightly than it had a moment ago? Her heart yearned to burst out of the ceiling and run to her. 'You know I've always said that I'll help you find King Dragon. Well, this is our best clue so far. I won't let you lose it, I won't let you lose hope. Wherever he is, if King Dragon's still alive, we'll find him. If we have to, we'll rescue him, and Baba and all the other dragons too!'

'Oh, my,' said Queen Dragon suddenly. 'Oh my, Lily!'

Lily paused for breath, her passionate speech interrupted. Across the room, Queen Dragon's mosaic eyes were staring at her, the black glass stark against the yellow.

'What's the matter, Queen Dragon? Is something wrong?'

'Don't you realise?' Queen Dragon's voice was wobbly with shock. 'Lily—you just moved your hand!'

In the magicians' ceiling, the magical creatures were having a conference. The subject under debate was Lily's hand. Had it moved? The general feeling was that Queen Dragon had been mistaken, but the discussion was long and heated, as might be expected in a place where there was so little other amusement. A few hopeful individuals thought there might be a chance that Queen Dragon had glimpsed something unusual, and the unicorns, when they spoke at all, appeared to accept her story. However, the unicorns were generally agreed to be totally mad, and even Lily was doubtful, for she had not been able to repeat what she had done. Only Queen Dragon was adamant that she had seen what she had seen. One thing was certain: it was the most exciting thing that had happened in the ceiling for centuries.

'But what did you do?' insisted the phoenix. 'You must know what you did, girl. Didn't you feel something?'

'Nothing,' said Lily. 'I wasn't aware I was doing anything. I was just reaching out for Queen Dragon.'

'Did anyone notice where her hand was when she came in?' asked a centaur. He seemed the most intelligent of the group, for he had asked sensible questions and stopped the others from asking silly ones. The centaur was not disbelieving, but he was cautious. Lily found herself rather liking him.

'Of course I didn't notice,' sniffed the griffin. 'Why would I trouble myself to look at *her*?'

'Maybe,' snapped Queen Dragon, 'because you were too busy listening to the sound of your own voice.'

'Hoity-toity.'

'Don't you hoity-toity me, *bird brain*.'

'Upstart!' yelled the griffin. 'In case it has escaped your notice, I have been in this ceiling for longer than anyone. Almost two thousand years, to be precise; in fact, it may safely be said that I am the last griffin in existence. That gives me a certain authority, *snake head*. And I say you're wrong about seeing her move. It's impossible. Can't be done.'

'All right,' said the centaur. 'No rank-pulling. We're all in this together. Lily, what do you think? *Could* you have moved your hand?'

'Queen Dragon thinks so,' said Lily.

'Queen Dragon could be wrong,' the centaur pointed out.

'Perhaps,' said Lily. 'But she's usually right. I trust her more than anyone else in the world. It's true I am only a human. But I am a Quench. My family has spent centuries pursuing dragons, and there's a bit of dragon in all of us as a result. Maybe that's the bit of me that hasn't been totally imprisoned by the spell.'

'Well, I can't say I see the sense in that,' said the centaur. 'Almost every creature here is a magical mixture. Look at me. I'm half human, half horse, yet I can't move a hairsbreadth.'

'It's not exactly the same,' said Lily. As she spoke, things started clicking into place. 'You see, centaurs and griffins were created magical. Humans weren't. That's what makes me different. And if the magicians used a spell that was intended for an ordinary human…well, it might not work properly on me.'

A little ripple went around the ceiling. 'Impossible.' 'I don't understand.' 'The girl's cracked.'

'You might be right,' said the centaur, and his voice was loud enough to cut across the ruckus and silence the others. 'But the question is this, Lily. Why haven't you been able to do it again?'

'I don't know.' Lily thought back over what had happened. She remembered how she had been upset, how she had wanted to reach out and comfort Queen Dragon. Lily tried to bring the moment back. She thought of Queen Dragon weeping over her lost love, of poor damaged Baba in her pyramid. If only she could help them! Suddenly Lily realised her fingers felt different from the rest of her body. They felt thick and heavy, and as she concentrated all her mental and physical energy down her arms—

A shocked gasp broke out from the rest of the ceiling as Lily slowly wriggled both her hands. This time no one argued whether they had moved or not. Lily curled her fingers and forced them forward. Very slowly, they slid through the ceiling, glass against glass, squeaking slightly as they went. Then all at once there was a strange sensation, as if she had popped through a membrane. Lily's fingers tingled, and with a sense of shocked delight she realised that they were no longer in the ceiling, no longer made of glass. They were flesh and blood, poking down through the mosaic into the room below.

'My goodness,' said the centaur softly. 'Will you look at that.'

'It should be easier now.' Lily tried again, first with her right hand, then with her left. Bit by bit, like the last squirt of toothpaste being squeezed from a tube, her hands pushed out of the ceiling into the banqueting hall. Her wrists, then her forearms, and finally her elbows, followed. But then, just as she reached the bit of her arm above her elbow, she suddenly stopped.

'I'm stuck!' Lily panted. 'Oh, no! What am I going to do?'

Her arms had gone as far as they could go. Try as she might, she could not force them out of the ceiling any further. She was trapped.

Ten

THE BATTLE OF THE BANQUETING HALL

'Help!' Lily cried. 'Somebody! Help me!'

'Pull back!' said the centaur urgently. 'You've proved you can do it, Lily. Pull back!'

'I—I can't!' And indeed, Lily could not. Her arms were stuck as firmly as if they were set in concrete. Try as she might, she could neither force them out of the ceiling any further, nor pull them back into the mosaic. They had stopped right where the scaly part of her arms gave way to ordinary skin, the right one above the wrist, the left one slightly above the elbow.

'I told you it was a stupid idea,' said the griffin in a panic. 'You silly girl! Now you'll get us all into trouble!' A swirl of fear ran around the ceiling. The creatures started babbling, then shouting, and the unicorns whinnied madly until Lily could hardly hear a thing for the rumpus in her head. She lifted her hands to her mosaic ears, but could not blot out a word of the telepathic babble.

'Lily! Are you all right?' Queen Dragon shouted.

'I think so.' But Lily knew it was not all right. Her arms felt constricted and her blood pounded painfully in her fingertips. A horrible thought occurred to her. How long could her arms dangle down into the room before they got gangrene and fell off? Even if that didn't happen, she was sure to be discovered the moment the magicians returned to the banqueting hall. Lily had only a vague idea of how much time had passed since her arrival in the ceiling. She had been so dazed and shocked it could have been hours before she had come to herself. But the table on the dais below her appeared to have been set for another meal, and that suggested the magicians were not far away.

'Hold on, Lily,' said Queen Dragon. 'We'll think of a way to rescue you.' The griffin snorted and the unicorns whinnied, but Lily was grateful for the lie. Gradually the outcry from the other creatures faded away. There was nothing more for them to say, and Lily knew that really they were frightened and trying to pretend they knew nothing about what was happening.

Time ticked away. It was hard for Lily to tell how long she dangled there, but her arms started to cramp painfully and go numb. She flexed her fingers grimly to try and keep the blood circulating, but it was hard work, and she could not help feeling frightened and depressed. From time to time Queen Dragon spoke to her, but even she soon ran out of encouragement. When the door eventually opened Lily was almost at the point of despair. She had hoped against hope it might be Roger, but instead it turned out to be Quin.

Quin went to the fire and stood pretending to warm her hands in front of its heatless blaze. Lily held her arms close to her body and kept as still as possible. She knew it was too much to hope that Quin wouldn't notice her predicament. Sure enough, after a moment's reflection, she chanced to look up and did.

'Well, well, well. Lily Quench.' Quin stepped onto the dais and walked along to the spot where Lily's arm was dangling just above Joscelin's chair. If she'd reached up, Lily could've touched her. 'I see you've had a busy day. I thought my spells had more...grip.'

'*Get lost.*' Lily flung her thought as furiously as she could project it. As she did, the double doors at the end of the hall opened again, admitting Roger and Joscelin. Roger looked disturbed, Joscelin plainly angry. He took one glance at Lily, then rounded on Quin.

'What's the meaning of this? I thought you said you'd imprisoned her.'

'It's only her arms, Joscelin.' Quin fell back a pace, alarmed. Her voice shook. 'I didn't count on the scales, that's all.'

'Then do something about it.' Joscelin sat down at the head of the table, right below Lily. He shook out his napkin. 'Have her arms cut off, straight after dinner. She won't have any more need for them where she is. Roast beef!'

'Bouillabaisse,' said Roger. 'What about you, Quin?'

'Oh, anything,' said Quin, glaring at Lily. A peacock appeared on her plate, like the one she had eaten the night before. She sat down in a huff, stabbed the peacock once with her fork, then pushed it aside.

'Well, that's torn it,' said the griffin, in the ceiling. 'You're going to look mighty silly without arms, girl.'

'Leave her alone!' Queen Dragon snapped, and the griffin made a sort of clucking noise and shut up. The rest of the creatures were quiet too. Lily herself felt sick. No terror she had been through yet, not even the water-filled dungeon at Mote Ely Castle, or Skellig Mor, where she had nearly been eaten alive by hungry sea dragons, had been quite as bad as this. Lily thought of her celebrated ancestor, Matilda Quench the Drakescourge. What would she have done in her position? *Make the most of things,* Matilda's voice seemed to say in her head. *Use your imagination, girl.* But Lily's imagination seemed to have seized up like a rusty machine.

It's being half Cornstalk, she thought mournfully. *I'm not a proper Quench at all. Matilda Drakescourge would have known exactly what to do.*—*Not always, Lily,* Matilda's voice replied, and suddenly a picture of Matilda came into Lily's head. It was not the Matilda she had met at Mote Ely Castle, but a girl about her own age, with spots and buck teeth, wearing an impractical long blue dress. She was standing in a field with a battered shield on her arm, and she was swishing at the grass with a sword. As Lily watched, she lost her balance and fell flat on her face. The vision faded. As it did, a great truth dawned on Lily: that Matilda, like Mad Brian and all the other famous Quenches of their line, had once been just as young and scared as she was now. It was by passing through trials such as the one she was enduring now, that they had learned to become intrepid and strong.

Lily looked down and saw that the magicians had reached their toast.

'To us,' Joscelin said. 'Long life and health.'

He lifted his crystal tumbler. It was only for a second, but the chance was there and Lily seized it. She dropped her left hand, grabbed the glass from Joscelin's fingers and tipped its contents violently over his head.

The next three seconds were among the most terrifying of Lily's life. All sorts of things started happening at once. The potion exploded against Joscelin's skin with a burst of red and black smoke; he let out a howl of agony, clutched his face and fell to the floor. As his grip on the pyramid's magic relaxed, Lily felt herself falling forward out of the mosaic. Her flattened face and body expanded like a rapidly inflating balloon and then she parted company with the ceiling and plunged uncontrollably downwards. Lily hit the table with a smash of crockery and wine glasses, heard Quin shriek and drop her own glass and Roger roar in fury. The walls of the pyramid shimmered and shook, and in the brief seconds of confusion, the imprisoned creatures came tumbling out of the ceiling into the room.

'Get her!' shouted Roger. Spectral hands snatched at Lily's clothes and she pulled away from them, rolling off the dining room table and taking the tablecloth and a silver salver with her. A candlestick fell with a clunk, and she heard

roars and screams of pain and anger as a giant free-for-all broke out among the creatures from the ceiling. After centuries of imprisonment, they had gone berserk. The manticore roared and leaped over the table, the unicorns screamed and ran wild, knocking down anything that got in their way with their flying hooves. One of them gored a minotaur in front of Lily's eyes and careered from the room, dripping blood. The griffin flapped its wings and screeched like a demented cockerel. Meanwhile phoenixes, squonks and all sorts of horrible and not-so-horrible creatures were running amok and attempting to wreak vengeance on their human captors. Only Queen Dragon remained in the ceiling, unable to free herself from the mosaic.

'Queen Dragon!'

'I'm trapped, Lily! I'm trapped!' Queen Dragon's head jerked wildly from side to side on her snaky neck. The rest of her was still in the ceiling, too big by far to fit into the room. Smoke streamed from her nostrils and there was a spatter of orange sparks. One hit the wall hangings and sizzled into flame.

'Fire!'

Something heavy dropped out of the ceiling onto the table. Lily started out from under the chair where she had dived to escape the unicorn, then stopped when she heard Queen Dragon scream. 'Lily! Close your eyes! It's a basilisk! If you look at it, it will turn you to stone!'

A dark scaly shape moved on the side of Lily's vision. Lily saw the griffin's eyes grow wide where it stood in front of her, and a look of unspeakable terror cross its face. Then it froze, unable to move. A greyish tinge swept rapidly over its bronze feathers and its bright eyes dulled in an instant.

'It's been turned to stone!' Queen Dragon shouted. 'Get out, Lily! Get out of this room before it's too late!'

Lily squirmed out from under the chair, slapped her fingers over her eyes and ran blundering for the door. It opened with a single shove of her hand. At once she found herself in total darkness. All the magical illumination had failed and the air was rent with horrible echoing cries. They were like nothing Lily had ever heard in her life, and for an instant she quailed and almost ran back. Then she remembered her torch was still in her pocket. With trembling hands, Lily took it out and turned it on.

The tiny light gave her just enough courage to continue. Lily ran down the corridor, invisible hands flapping at her face as she went, the screams following her like a thousand lost and mourning spirits. 'Go away!' she shouted furiously. 'Leave me be!' The cries faded and she was able to go on. The unicorn that had run out earlier came galloping past along the passage, its horn smashed and hanging bleeding from its forehead. A flock of grey hands came fluttering out of the darkness like moths, and the floor teemed with rats, mice and beetles, all racing for the exit, as if they were escaping a sinking ship.

Lily recognised the passage that led to the entrance and ran into it. The stone door at the bottom was gaping open. On the downward slope she tripped and fell, grazing her knee, but she was up and running again in an instant. There was moonlight ahead of her and fresh night air blowing into the musty darkness. Lily barged through the open door and cried out with relief.

'Help!' She stumbled down two or three steps, paused, and shouted again at the top of her lungs.

'Somebody! Please, help me!' A dragonish moan sounded somewhere in the darkness below her. Lily ran down the steps two at a time. A great black shape loomed up in front of her. She screamed and dropped her torch, then caught a flash of green in the light of its rolling beam.

'Baba!' Lily snatched up her torch. 'Baba! You've got to help us! Queen Dragon is trapped inside the pyramid! She's in the ceiling and there's a basilisk, and the magicians—'

'Joscelin's magic faltered.' Baba seemed dazed. 'My pyramid collapsed. I don't understand.' A look of fear came into her eyes. 'I don't know what to do.'

'You must help us! Help Sinhault! Baba, we have to do something before they find us again!' But as she spoke, Lily realised instinctively that it was hopeless. After three thousand years of imprisonment, Baba's freedom had come too late.

A bright light suddenly appeared behind Lily and she wheeled to face it. Joscelin stood on the pyramid steps. His face was hideously burned, his hair singed, his clothes ruined. Lily stumbled back towards Baba. There was nothing she could do, nowhere she could run. He was going to kill her and Baba, and then there would be nothing and no one to save Queen Dragon.

Joscelin lifted his staff and advanced on her menacingly. Then Baba opened her mouth and, quite unexpectedly, began to sing.

Eleven

BABA'S SONG

The note that poured from Baba's throat was pure and terrible. It was a cry for help, the most desperate call a dragon could make, for it was the Dragons' Cry of Summoning. In their hour of greatest need any dragon might utter it and count upon the help of all dragons within earshot. Used carelessly, when no dragon was near to help, the Cry of Summoning could rebound on the caller and kill her. It made mountains shake and hills quiver. It pierced to the vaults of heaven and to the uttermost depths of the sea.

Joscelin took a step backwards. From the expression on his face Lily knew that he recognised the cry. He looked terrified. For thousands of years Baba had been his prisoner and he had known himself to be safe, for no other dragon had been close enough for her to attempt to summon them. But now, Queen Dragon was in the pyramid. Baba was calling her out, and the air was thick with a powerful magic, the magic that was instilled into every dragon before it was born, that was purer and stronger than anything any human magician could encompass.

Joscelin raised his staff and started to shout his own incantation, but the Cry of Summoning drowned out his voice. Still, the long notes issued from Baba's throat. She staggered a little and closed her eyes. Black drops of blood stood out upon her forehead. The Cry of Summoning was starting to come back on her.

Lily started running towards Joscelin. She felt his magic curl around her feet, slowing her down and bringing her to a stop. Baba raised herself up on her forelegs and threw back her head, and without warning her song abruptly changed. Now she was singing not one, but two songs: the Cry of Summoning and, twining around it in mysterious harmony, an ancient dragonish song that was somehow strangely familiar to Lily's ears.

The effect was immediate and electrifying. There was an answering scream from within the pyramid, followed by a deafening rumble as Queen Dragon exploded through the stonework, spraying rubble and fire everywhere. Lily dropped to the ground. She had just enough presence of mind to pull her fireproof cape over her head as Queen Dragon swept overhead, screaming angrily. Fire rained down and she heard Joscelin's screams cut off suddenly as he was caught and vaporised. But she dared not look. Lily smelled the smoke and felt the hideous heat swell to almost unbearable levels. She heard Baba cry out and fall heavily to the ground as if she had collapsed. The ground shook and the air filled with dust, as the pyramids fell into ruins around her. Then the attack was over. The heat faded, the smoke and vapour cleared. Lily lifted her shaking body from the ground and saw Queen

Dragon wheel overhead and come in to land beside them.

'Lily!'

'I'm all right, Queen Dragon. I'm not hurt.' Lily turned to Baba, who lay slumped on the blackened earth not far away. Her flaking eyelids were closed and she was unconscious, her breath coming in shallow, painful snatches. The Cry of Summoning had spent the last of her strength.

'Baba!' Queen Dragon folded her leathery wings. Tears rained down her face and hissed as they hit the smoking earth. She sat down at Baba's side and laid her crimson claw over Baba's faded one, looking for all the world, thought Lily, like two old ladies holding hands. Baba's green colour had faded to a sickly wash and her breathing grew even harsher and slower than it had been before. A few spot fires from Queen Dragon's attack still smoked in the soggy grass around them, but as Lily pulled her fireproof cape around her, and huddled up close to Queen Dragon's side, they began to go out, one by one.

A great rattle sounded in Baba's throat. She twitched painfully, then unexpectedly opened her eyes.

'Sinhault. I'm sorry.'

'Don't be sorry, Baba.' Queen Dragon tightened her claw. 'I'm here, now. You don't have to speak if you don't want to.'

'But I do want to.' Baba looked at her pleadingly. 'There's so much to tell you. So many things I wish I hadn't done. I want your forgiveness.'

'Forgiveness?' Queen Dragon was puzzled. 'But what for, Baba? What could you have possibly done to me?'

'I am a traitor,' said Baba simply. 'I stopped King Dragon from returning to the Great War of the Dragons.'

Beside Queen Dragon, Lily sat quiet as a mouse. There was a long silence. Three thousand years would not have been enough to fill it.

'You want to know how I did it?' said Baba. 'Well. You are the first to hear. I smashed the Eye Stone to stop them from going back.'

'You smashed the Eye Stone?' whispered Queen Dragon.

'Yes.'

'And King Dragon? Is he…alive?'

'I believe he is,' said Baba. 'In my heart, I hope

so. I know Joscelin has tried to find him, but King Dragon and his companions have passed beyond the fastnesses of this world. No human magic has been able to track them down. For a long time I thought they must have died, but then one night I had a dream. It was so real, I knew it must be true. Our friends were in a valley, far to the north-west, beyond the limits of all the maps that were ever made. It was a magical place. They were safe there. When I woke up I was so happy for them that it didn't seem to matter I could never rejoin them.' The tears stood in her eyes. 'The magicians blamed me for letting them escape. You see, I alone of our company had listened to everything they said and believed them. They had offered to help stop the battle, but only if we stayed at the pyramids and helped with what Joscelin called their research. They said there was no need to hurry because the Eye Stone could take us back to the start of the battle whenever we chose. King Dragon didn't trust them. He decided to leave secretly under cover of darkness.

'I was in a panic. You see, I didn't believe King Dragon could stop the war without the magicians' help. I smashed the Eye Stone and flew straight to Joscelin. The others tried to escape by flying away. The magicians went after them, fought them with spells. Balefire's wings had been scorched in the battle. He couldn't fly properly, and they brought him down with magic nets and killed him.' Tears seeped out from under Baba's cracked and blackened eyelids. One washed against Lily's foot; it was barely warm. 'He died because of me, Sinhault. It was my fault. Snaketongue was Balefire's friend; he cursed me as they flew away. They left me behind—because I betrayed them.'

'You didn't betray them, Baba,' said Queen Dragon. 'You were tricked.'

'Only because I wanted to be.' Baba wept. 'Sinhault, I am so ashamed. Joscelin told me he would make me the most powerful dragon in the world. That I would be stronger and more powerful than King Dragon, more beautiful than Annacondia. And I believed him. I believed every word they said because I wanted to. And when I went to them to claim their promises, they cut off my wings and laughed, and threw me into the darkness. Oh, I am well punished for what I did! Many times I thought my heart would break under the grief of it. But I was young and strong and despite my torment I lived on, forsaken and forgotten. Our kind die hard, Sinhault, and I have borne more than most.'

'And borne it bravely.' Queen Dragon searched for the right thing to say. 'The world of the dragons has ended, Baba. It ended with the war in the Black Mountains. Nothing you could have said or done would have stopped it. You must not berate yourself for what you did. What does it matter now? Our kind is scattered, there is no country of the dragons anymore. The rest of us live, like you, almost completely alone.'

'Alone?' Baba struggled with this. 'What about your friends? Surely some of us survived the war. Do you still see Serpentine? Oh, I couldn't bear it if Serpentine Bridgestock was killed!'

'My friends are human now,' said Queen Dragon. 'I have learned human ways. But Serpentine's fine, Baba. She's fine.' Lily, who knew the truth about Serpentine's fate, felt something clutch inside her chest.

'I'm glad.' Baba sighed. 'I'm tired, Sinhault. I can't talk anymore. I think I'll go to sleep now.

Will you sing to me? Sing the song King Dragon wrote. Sing about the country of the dragons at the beginning of the world.'

'Of course.' Queen Dragon bowed her head and collected herself. She hummed a few notes, and the hum became a song. Lily recognised it, for it was the one Baba herself had sung when she had called Queen Dragon forth from the pyramid. It was a lament for all that the dragons had lost, for the homeland that they would never see again.

There were many verses. Lily listened to them all, though she could not understand a word of the dragon language in which it was sung. At last Queen Dragon's voice grew hoarse with singing and it came upon Lily that she was the only one listening. For in the darkness Baba had grown cold and her fire had gone out. Already, a semblance of stone was creeping over her flesh. The green scales were dull and there was a little chill in the air that there had not been before.

The last notes of Queen Dragon's song faded out into darkness and cold air. She bowed her head, and for several minutes sat slumped forward and silent. Lily stood beside her. At last, with an enormous effort, Queen Dragon roused herself.

'Stand back, Lily,' she said.

Lily walked away and stood watching. Queen Dragon closed her eyes. She arched her neck and a stream of fire shot from her nostrils, engulfing Baba's body in flame.

The heat was so great that Lily could not watch. She turned aside and lifted her cape to protect her face as the dragonfire continued to pour forth. For a moment, through the folds of fabric, she thought she saw something moving in the flame, like wings of fire uplifted in flight. But the sight was too dreadful to bear and she closed her eyes again, half-blinded, until at last with a huge rushing sound the great skeleton collapsed in on itself, and it was ended.

The heat abated and the smoke drifted up. Lily dropped her cape and opened her eyes. Baba was gone, and Queen Dragon sat, covered in ash among the ruins of the pyramids, with great boiling tears coursing down her scaly face.

Twelve

ROGER

Evangeline had returned to Ashby Castle in a thoughtful mood. It was very late and her head was full of questions that refused to be answered. Why had Murdo been so frightened? Why had he refused to speak to her? Did he know who Manuelo was? Evangeline was deeply puzzled. She was sure something didn't quite fit, but for the life of her, she could not work out what it was.

She found the king in the library with a pile

of ancient books, drinking a mug of cocoa. A small saucepan was warming on the library fire, waiting for her arrival. As soon as she came in, Lionel poured out some cocoa for her and handed her a tin of shortbread.

'I've been looking up some histories of the Black Empire,' he said. 'I'm trying to find out whether any of the Black Counts was called Manuelo.'

Evangeline folded her hands around the warm mug. 'Any luck?'

'No.' Lionel sighed. 'Three Gordons. One Bradley. Two Felixes and a Raymond. There's certainly nothing to account for Gordon calling himself Manuelo. How was Murdo?'

'Frightened.' Evangeline thoughtfully sipped her cocoa. 'He'd certainly heard of Manuelo when I mentioned the name. What I don't know is whether he was afraid *of* him—or *for* him.'

'For him, surely,' said Lionel. 'If he's Gordon, that is.'

'I'm not sure that he is Gordon,' confessed Evangeline. 'Lionel, do you have Manuelo's cloak handy? I'd like to have another look at it.'

Lionel went over to a box in the corner.

He took out the intruder's cloak and gave it to the queen. She shook out its folds and looked at it carefully.

'This hem's been wet.'

'It's been raining for the last couple of days.' Lionel thought a moment. 'But not on the night of the robbery. I remember hearing the sprinklers going in the Botanic Gardens before I went to bed.'

'Interesting.' Evangeline lifted the cloak to her nose and sniffed. She ran her hands over the folds of cloth. At the bottom, just above the hem at the back of the cloak, she stopped. For a moment she worked away delicately at the fabric, and then one long finger appeared through the wool like a worm popping up out of an apple.

'This cloak's been ripped on something. Look.'

'That doesn't mean anything,' objected Lionel. 'It's an old cloak. There are lots of holes in it.'

'Yes. But the other holes are all patched. See, here.' Evangeline pointed out the mends. 'Whoever owned this cloak was particular about their clothes. When it tore, he repaired it promptly. Yet he didn't have time to fix this hole. That doesn't mean it happened on the night of the robbery—but it must have happened not very long before.'

'I still don't see how knowing this can help us,' said Lionel.

'It helps, because it tells us more about the sort of person Manuelo is,' said Evangeline. 'Think of what we know about Gordon. Is he the sort of boy who would sit and darn his clothes? I don't think so. And there's something else, too. Look at this cloak, Lionel. Why would anyone in their right mind wear something as heavy as this in Ashby at this time of year? It's the sort of thing you'd wear in a snowstorm, or when you were flying on Queen Dragon's head.'

'You'd wear it if you came from the Black Mountains,' said Lionel. 'It's cold there, especially at this time of year.'

'Yes,' said Evangeline grimly. 'But what I'm wondering, is whether Manuelo came to Ashby from a place *where it wasn't this time of year.*'

Lionel stared at her. Evangeline met his gaze, and nodded. The king's friendly face grew stern under his mop of curls and he shoved back his chair.

'Right. I'm going straight to the dungeons.'

'So am I.' Evangeline drained the last of her cocoa, and stood up. She followed the king out of the room and down the stairs, out into the castle bailey. Together they crossed to the gatehouse and let themselves into the old dungeons.

'We've been following a red herring,' said Lionel, as they walked along the whitewashed passage towards the vaults. 'We've been so obsessed with that secret tunnel we've forgotten that no one ever saw the intruder coming from or heading in that direction. You know what? I think Manuelo never even knew the tunnel existed. I think he's found another way in, a way none of us have even thought of.'

'This is the vault where I fought the intruder,' said Evangeline. They stopped in front of a door and Lionel produced a key. It took him a moment to unlock the three locks which secured it, then the heavy door swung open and they turned on the light.

The Treasure of Mote Ely consisted of jewellery, armour, and other precious items made of gold and silver. Actual cash was the least, yet for Ashby's purposes the most useful part of it.

This was the vault where the coin was kept: gold crowns and silver dragons and other unknown coins from the distant past. It had been sorted out into canvas money bags, filling two whole walls of the vault. The bags were stacked on shelves and there was a table and a wooden chair on the back wall.

'That table has been moved,' said Evangeline immediately. 'It's standing crookedly against the wall.' She went over and examined it more closely. 'Look, Lionel. Footprints. You can just make them out beside the chair.' She pulled the chair away, and the king crouched down beside them.

'Strange. It looks like our intruder was wearing gumboots. They were wet, too. There are little bits of mud that have stuck to the floor.'

'Look!' Evangeline cried. She pulled out her torch and shone it over the wall. A tiny tuft of material was protruding from between two stones. 'It's wool from the intruder's cloak! It must have caught on his way into the vault. We've found another secret entrance!'

'And here's the catch that opens it.' Lionel inserted his finger into a crack and pushed down.

A section of wall moved aside, just big enough for one person to creep into. 'It's exactly the same mechanism as the dungeon entrance to the other tunnel. I wonder where it leads?' He took Evangeline's torch and stepped through into the darkness on the other side, then helped the queen in after him. Lionel swept the torch beam over the walls. They were in a low tunnel, barely big enough to stand up in. It was made of ancient-looking bricks with an arched roof, and the ground was covered with an evil-smelling film of brackish water.

'Careful, Evie,' said the king. 'This could be slippery.' He took her hand firmly, and they walked a little way along the passage, shining the torch beam back and forth as they went.

'This isn't a tunnel,' said Evangeline. 'It's an old drain. It must be the one I read about in that book. Where do you think we are now?'

'Hard to say,' said Lionel. 'Somewhere under the old moat, I think. It was emptied and grassed over in my grandparent's time. They thought Ashby was so peaceful, it would never be needed again. The reclaimed land was given to the Botanic

Gardens. At a guess, we're somewhere underneath them.'

'This water must have backed up from the Ashby Canal, then,' said Evangeline. 'We've had a lot of rain over the last few months and it's very full.'

'Maybe,' said Lionel. He suddenly stopped, his torch beam fixed on a round hole in the middle of the wall ahead. It was dark and mysterious looking, and around its rim were carved several strokes, like the lashes of an oversized eye.

'Watch out, Evie!' he shouted. 'It's an Eye Stone!'

'Well. It looks like that's the end of our quest,' said Lily to Queen Dragon. They were sitting in the middle of the ruined complex of pyramids, waiting for the sun to come up. Lily felt depressed. She had been through terrible dangers before, but this was the first time one of her quenching expeditions had actually failed.

In the lap of her dress was a large diamond she had found in the ashes, the tip of Joscelin's staff.

The diamond was so large it would have been worth a king's ransom, but Lily would not have kept it at any price. She drew back her arm and hurled it as far and as hard as she could into the darkness. There was a satisfying plunk as it fell into one of the streams. Lily hoped it would lie there until the end of the world.

'Don't get too depressed, Lily,' said Queen Dragon. 'There's always another way. We'll find it, somewhere. Think of it like this. Between them, those three magicians have wreaked more evil than an entire dynasty of Black Counts. I did not mean to kill them or wreck their pyramid, but I'm satisfied the world will be a safer place without them.'

'I guess so,' said Lily despondently. 'The problem is, there's so little time left. Gordon could be invading Ashby as we speak. And now that the magicians are dead, we'll never find out where the Eye Stones are.'

'Maybe we won't need to,' said Queen Dragon. 'I've been thinking about something, Lily. When Joscelin was attacked, his magic faltered and you were able to fall out of the ceiling. When he died, the pyramids he made collapsed. Well,

Suppose that goes for all the magicians' magic? What if their magic dies when they do?'

'You mean, when the pyramid collapsed on Roger and Quin, the Eye Stones stopped working?' Lily looked at Queen Dragon wonderingly. 'Queen Dragon, do you really think that could be right?'

'The only way to be sure is to go and check,' said Queen Dragon practically. 'Come on, Lily. It's light enough to leave now. Let's get moving and find out.'

Lily dusted off her skirts and clambered up onto her accustomed place on Queen Dragon's head. It was hard not to feel relieved that she was leaving the pyramids forever. Queen Dragon sprang into the air. A few wingstrokes brought them to the ring of Eye Stones surrounding the pyramids. The circle was now in ruins, with some stones still standing, others lying toppled over and broken. Lily saw her camping things, clothes, blankets and provisions, lying where she had left them, just beyond it.

'We'll just pop down and fetch your gear,' said Queen Dragon. She wheeled around in the sky and came in to land. But as she neared the ground, she suddenly lurched off course. Lily grabbed hold of her harness to avoid being pitched off.

'What happened?'

'I don't know.' Queen Dragon flew laboriously around again. But when she reached the spot near the campsite, the same thing happened. An invisible barrier had pushed her backwards, forcing her back inside the ring of stones.

'This isn't the Eye Stones,' said Queen Dragon. 'It's some other magic. I've got a bad feeling...'

'But you said—' Lily broke off as she realised what the barrier meant. One of the magicians must still be alive. She looked out across the ruined field of pyramids and pointed. 'Queen Dragon! The observatory is still standing. Roger must have survived the Great Pyramid's collapse!'

'He must have escaped in the confusion,' said Queen Dragon in a panic. 'Oh, dear. What are we going to do now?'

'We could try and talk him into letting us go. Roger wasn't all that bad, Queen Dragon. In fact, in a way he was quite nice.'

'Roger may have had better manners, but he's still a magician,' retorted Queen Dragon. 'Bad is bad, Lily, no matter what pretty clothes it wears. Don't you realise? By now he'll be desperate. That potion was all that was keeping him alive. That means he'll be looking for a dragon. And the only dragon he knows about is—'

'You.' Suddenly Lily realised what a fool she had been. 'He's trying to keep you inside the boundary! Queen Dragon, what are we going to do?'

'I don't know.' Queen Dragon sounded truly terrified. She flapped around, veering from one side of the circle to the other like a demented goldfish swimming around and around its bowl. 'Lily, we've got to get out! We've got to get out! Oh no. It's too late. Look, he's coming!'

She turned in mid-air and started flapping furiously away from an object that had suddenly appeared in the sky in front of them. Lily whipped her sword out of its sheath. Its blade glinted red in the dawn light. For the first time in all her expeditions she felt like she was going to need it.

Roger was coming straight at them, faster than she could have believed possible. And he was flying on a pair of green dragon wings, swinging a golden net above his head...

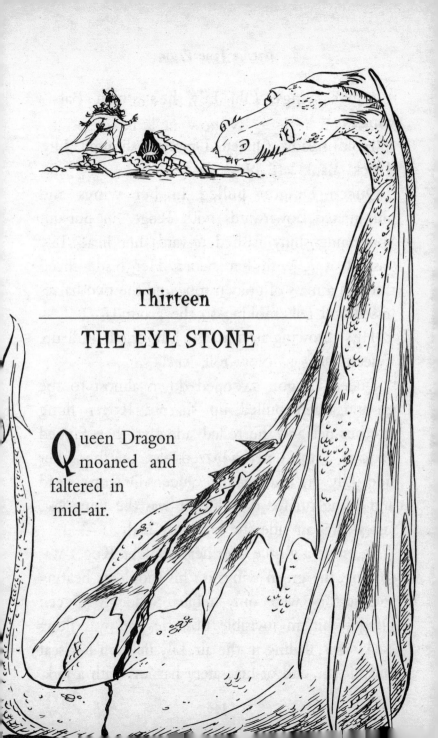

Thirteen

THE EYE STONE

Queen Dragon moaned and faltered in mid-air.

'Baba's wings! Oh, Lily, he's stolen Baba's wings!'

'Hold steady, Queen Dragon!' shouted Lily. 'Duck! Bank left! Now *dive*!'

Queen Dragon pulled in her wings and plummeted downwards with Roger in pursuit. Something shiny flashed towards her head. Lily slashed at it with her sword. Her blade sliced through a mass of golden rope and the two halves hissed and fell smoking to the ground.

'He's throwing nets at us!' Lily cried. 'Pull up, Queen Dragon! Now roll, *hard*!'

Queen Dragon swooped down almost to the ground, then pulled up sharply. Roger flung another net and she rolled sideways, then flipped back as a third net whizzed past on the other side. Lily lay flat against Queen Dragon's head and clung on for dear life. It was the bumpiest, fastest dragon ride she had ever had.

She stole a glance over her shoulder. Roger was gaining, the green wings on his shoulders beating so fast they were only a blur. Suddenly Queen Dragon hit an invisible obstacle and was flung backwards, flailing in the air. Lily flew off her seat and hit the end of her safety harness with a jerk.

'*Queen Dragon!*' Lily flopped about, banging the side of Queen Dragon's head like a string bag full of onions. Her helmet slipped to one side and she struggled to straighten it. 'What's happening? I can't see! *Ouch!*' But Queen Dragon was unable to do anything. She righted herself and whizzed over Roger's pyramid, bumped into the barrier on the other side, and flew back like a fly in a bottle. With an enormous effort, Lily managed to push back her helmet and claw her way back up her harness into her seat. A third time, Queen Dragon banged into the invisible barrier. Now Lily could see what Roger was doing. He was slowly, deliberately pulling the barrier inward, giving Queen Dragon less and less room in which to fly.

A spatter of small fireballs sizzed past her head like deadly fireworks. Lily ducked and batted at them with her sword. She managed to hit one and it exploded with a loud bang that almost blew her weapon from her grasp.

'*Ow!*' Lily snatched back her hand. The sword blade glowed hot for an instant and she juggled its leather hilt from one hand to the next. 'That was *nasty!*'

'You're telling me!' Queen Dragon yelped, as another fireball exploded on her flank. 'Ouch! Ouch! *Ouch!*' A series of fireballs peppered her left side and she dived unexpectedly, almost throwing Lily off again. 'Lily! He's going for my wings! If he hits me, we're finished! *Aaah!*'

Queen Dragon screamed with pain. She floundered in mid-air and started going down like a giant red zeppelin. Lily glimpsed a ragged, bleeding hole in her left wing. Roger flew towards them, swinging another magic net above his head. For the first time, Lily caught a glimpse of his face. A long cut on his cheek had opened up and was bleeding, and his expression was murderous.

He hurled the net. Lily caught it in her sword, but it tangled in the blade and hissed around it like a nest of snakes.

'Flame him, Queen Dragon!' shouted Lily. 'Shoot him down!' She shook her sword frantically, and the deadly net finally dislodged. Queen Dragon threw back her head. Fire blasted from her nostrils, but Roger was ready for it. He lifted his hand and the dragonfire hit an invisible shield and streamed safely around him. Roger opened his mouth to laugh—and then, before the sound had a chance to come out, something totally unexpected happened.

Queen Dragon's jet of fire hit the invisible barrier close behind him. It roared, flared up— and bounced off straight into Roger's unprotected back. Baba's green wings went up in a flash of flame. White ash showered everywhere. Screaming and smoking, Roger fell out of the sky and hit the ground with a hideous thud.

Her heart pounding, Lily leaned over the side of Queen Dragon's head and tried to see where he had fallen.

'Is he still alive?'

'Of course he's alive.' Queen Dragon wheeled about and headed painfully for the observatory. 'His pyramid's still standing. All we've done is slow him down. Lily, I'm going to have to land. I can't keep flying much longer. Hold on tight!'

She cleared the observatory balustrade and landed on the terrace with a rending crash. Paving stones flew up like broken teeth and part of the balustrade collapsed. Lily unbuckled her harness and slid hastily down.

'Queen Dragon! Are you all right?' But Queen

Dragon clearly was not all right. Her golden eyes brimmed with tears of pain, and her left wing dragged limply across the terrace. She was hideously burned. Roger's fireballs had peppered her wing with scorch marks and the direct hit she had taken at the end had ripped a hole right through its leathery webbing. Dark, glistening sheets of blood ran down from the jagged wound and dripped onto the terrace. It smoked and pooled on the pavement at Lily's feet.

'I'll be fine, Lily,' Queen Dragon said faintly. 'I just won't be able to fly for a while, that's all. Is Roger still there?'

Lily looked over the broken balustrade. A dark shape lay on the ground a little distance away from the pyramid. 'He's not moving,' she reported. 'I think he must be unconscious.'

'An ordinary human would be dead,' said Queen Dragon, wincing. 'Lily, you're going to have to leave me here. As long as Roger's unconscious, the magical barrier won't be working. Put as much distance between yourself and this pyramid as you can. I don't want you to be around when Roger wakes up.'

'Queen Dragon! As if I'd leave you!' The words

had scarcely left Lily's mouth when Queen Dragon groaned and slumped down in a gigantic heap. The terrace creaked and sagged beneath her weight and a splash of blood flew up and hit Lily's fireproof cape. Lily gave a cry of alarm and started to run forward. Then a familiar voice spoke unexpectedly right at her feet and she screamed with fear.

'Where would you like to go?'

'Get away!' Lily whipped out her sword. Queen Dragon roused herself. There was a rattle of flame in her nostrils as she prepared to attack. But though Roger had seemingly spoken, he was not there. Only the sound of his voice floated up to Lily, speaking eerily out of the pavement at her feet.

'Where would you like to go?'

'Where are you?' Lily's eyes raced over the pavement. Amid the rubble where she was standing was the granite map table, broken in two and knocked aside. Lily caught a glimpse of something black lying in the depression where it had stood. It was a stone, set into the terrace and covered with a network of silver lines, radiating like lashes from a central eye.

An Eye Stone.

'I'm right here,' said the Eye Stone, in answer to Lily's question. It sounded slightly irritated. 'Where else would I be? Where would you—'

'I haven't decided.' Lily sheathed her sword and crouched cautiously beside it. 'Are you...*working*?'

'Of course I am,' said the Eye Stone. 'Didn't you set the spell yourself?'

'The spell?' Lily looked confused. But Queen Dragon nodded.

'The blood, Lily,' she said weakly. 'My blood. Look. It's all over the stone.'

'Dragon's blood! Of course!' Lily stared at the blood dripping into the depression. At Mote Ely she had learned how the Eye Stones' magic was controlled by smearing drops of dragon's blood on the stonework. Inadvertently, she and Queen Dragon had set this Eye Stone working. Lily did not like the thought of using it, and she was sure Queen Dragon felt the same. Nevertheless, it was still an escape route, an unexpected way home.

'Be careful, Lily,' warned Queen Dragon. 'I know what you're thinking. It could be dangerous. It could even be a trap.'

'I know,' said Lily. 'But we've got to get away

from here before Roger wakes up. What other choice do we have?' She spoke again to the Eye Stone, choosing her words with care. 'Tell me, Eye Stone. If I asked you to, could you take us home to Ashby?'

'Can you be more precise?' Roger's voice floated eerily up out of the pavement. 'Ashby's a big place. Where exactly do you want to go?'

'We've got a choice?' Queen Dragon was startled.

'There's a working Eye Stone in the marsh at Mote Ely,' Roger's voice replied. 'Another at Ashby Castle. If you tell me where you're going, I'll take you to the closest one.'

'Yes, of course,' Queen Dragon flustered. 'We're going—'

'Queen Dragon, stop!' exclaimed Lily. 'Wait! It can talk. Our quest. We can finish our quest. It can tell us where the other Eye Stones are!'

'Lily, you're right.' Queen Dragon shook herself. 'Eye Stone. Wait a moment. Before we decide where to go, can you tell us how many working Eye Stones there are left?'

'Only Roger's stones survive now,' replied the Eye Stone. 'There are seven of them. One at

Mote Ely on the borders of Ashby. One in the great drain beneath Ashby Castle. One at Dragon's Downfall which Roger shared with Quin and Joscelin…'

'Go slower, go slower!' Lily ticked the stones off on her fingers until she got to seven, then got the stone to repeat the list. At last, when she had it right, she climbed back onto Queen Dragon's head and strapped herself tightly into her harness.

'Ashby Castle!'

At Queen Dragon's command, the Eye Stone began to spin. A hole opened up in front of them and Lily and Queen Dragon tumbled in and began to fall.

At once everything went cold, silent and almost completely dark. It was like being in a glass tunnel, sliding out of control. Lily felt as if she could barely breathe. Terrified, she clung onto her helmet and closed her eyes. Beneath her, Queen Dragon moaned with fear.

Suddenly, the glassy tunnel began to shake around them. A deafening pounding started up somewhere ahead. Queen Dragon hit the wall and bounced off. Lily screamed. Something somewhere was going hideously wrong.

'What's happening, Queen Dragon? Is it Roger?'

'No!' Queen Dragon could barely make herself heard over the racket. 'Someone's trying to close the Eye Stone off at the other end! Hold on, Lily! We're almost there!'

Lily glimpsed a faint light and buried her face in Queen Dragon's scales. She felt like a stream of fizzy soft drink, about to shoot out of a bottle and be splattered everywhere. There was a terrible rending sound, as if stone was exploding all around them. A huge force ripped Lily out of her harness, turned her over and dropped her on the ground with a bone-jarring crash. Rocks fell all around her, bouncing tinnily off her helmet, and then she was hit by a huge shower of dust from above and realised she had arrived.

Lily sprawled, coughing and choking. For several moments she could hardly see a thing. Then her vision cleared and she glimpsed a crowd of people standing in front of her. There were workers with jackhammers and yellow safety helmets, all coughing and flapping their hands in front of their faces. Off to one side were two astonished, yet vaguely familiar faces. Lily pushed a mass of dust-encoated hair back out of her eyes and blinked. It was King Lionel and Queen Evangeline of Ashby, dressed in working clothes with earmuffs on their ears.

'My goodness, Lily,' said Lionel faintly. 'What an entrance.'

Lily scrambled shakily over a pile of rubble. Now that the dust was clearing, she saw that she was standing in the ruins of what looked like an ancient drain. Queen Dragon was behind her, squashed into the tunnel like a saveloy into a bun. Her head and shoulders poked out through an enormous hole where she had brought the roof down, and an ancient grommet, buried after the demolition of the factory, hung off the side of her head like a gigantic earring.

'Why, Lily, it's the Ashby Botanic Gardens!' she exclaimed. 'I can see my dragon house. The Eye Stone wasn't lying! We're home!'

'Just as well that treasure's still intact, Lionel,' remarked Evangeline. 'I can see this is going to be an expensive repair job.' Lily looked at her enquiringly. Queen Dragon's giant head poked down from above.

'Treasure? Are we talking about breakfast, by any chance?'

'Not exactly,' said Lionel. 'Queen Dragon, are you all right? Your wing looks like it's bleeding. Should I call a vet?'

'A vet?' Queen Dragon reared up indignantly. 'A *vet*? I'm a dragon, not a dachshund.'

'Well, if you're sure,' said the king doubtfully. 'In any case, we're very glad you're back. There's been rather a lot happening here in Ashby while you've been gone.'

'Oh?' Lily cocked an eyebrow.

'A mysterious robber from the Black Mountains who knows more about the Eye Stones and Gordon's plans than I care to think about,' explained Evangeline. 'I'm sorry, Lily. It looks like another quest.'

'Not until after I've eaten,' said Queen Dragon, firmly. 'I've got some nice car wrecks back at the dragon house. And after that, I'm going to have a little nap. Being flattened and shot at really takes it out of you.' She flipped the grommet expertly off her ear and swallowed it, then heaved herself out of the drain into the gardens and limped painfully away.

Lily climbed up a pile of fallen brickwork and watched her go. Behind her, the stone bulk of Ashby Castle stood bathed in the pink light of dawn, the pennants on its turrets lifting lazily in the breeze. In the green expanse of the gardens, the gardeners with their wheelbarrows and shovels were just starting work. A few of them stopped to greet Queen Dragon as she passed, and then her crimson bulk disappeared into the beehive-shaped structure of the dragon house.

Lily blinked. For a moment, an unexpected vision filled her eyes, a vision that brought Baba sharply to mind. In her anguish, Baba had dreamed of King Dragon in a faroff, magical valley, but for an instant Lily could have sworn she saw him here. His great gold shape glistened in the sunlight as he followed Queen Dragon across the grass, and when he reached the tunnel-shaped entrance to the dragon house, he paused and looked straight at Lily. The distance between them was suddenly as nothing. His golden eyes were bright with the wisdom of his four thousand years, and at the sight of his awesome beauty Lily felt suddenly frightened of what lay ahead. What would happen to her when Queen Dragon was reunited with her lost love? The thought was so painful it was all Lily could do not to weep. At that moment, the rising sun appeared over the roof of Ashby Church. Its golden rays struck King Dragon's scales, dazzling her eyes, and she dropped her gaze. When Lily lifted her eyes again, the vision was gone.

Lily looked down and saw that the workmen had gone. Lionel and Evangeline were waiting for her. The king stepped up onto the brickwork and reached out a hand to help her down.

'Come on, Lily,' he said. 'Let's go and have some breakfast.'

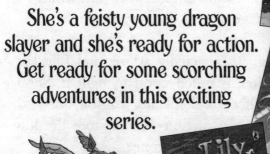

**Join Lily Quench on a
perilous mission**

LILY QUENCH AND
THE BLACK MOUNTAINS
NATALIE JANE PRIOR

In the Black Mountains there's nothing but snow,
ice and blizzards. But it's there that the magical
blue lily grows, and it's the only thing that can
help Lily Quench stop the evil Black Count from
invading her beloved homeland.

With her friend Queen Dragon, Lily embarks on a
perilous mission to bring the blue lily back to
Ashby. Captured and imprisoned, then befriended
by the count's son, Gordon, they flee to the eerie
heights of Dragon's Downfall…the place where
Lily and Queen Dragon must confront their
greatest fear.

**Quench your thirst for
adventure with Lily**

LILY QUENCH AND
THE TREASURE OF MOTE ELY
NATALIE JANE PRIOR

Kidnapped and taken back into the past to a
crumbling castle in the middle of a creepy marsh,
Lily Quench searches for the long lost treasure of
Mote Ely—and a way back to her own time.

Locked in a dungeon, attacked by a dragon and
befriended by her eccentric great-great-great-great
grandmother, Lily finds that enemies can sometimes
be friends—and that old friends can unexpectedly
turn into enemies.

**Fly with Lily on a dangerous and
thrilling journey**

LILY QUENCH AND THE
LIGHTHOUSE OF SKELLIG MOR
NATALIE JANE PRIOR

At the ends of the earth is Skellig Lir, a dreamy
magical island that is inhabited by mysterious
people with strange powers. To get there, Lily
Quench and Queen Dragon must brave magic,
storms and seas swarming with deadly sea
dragons—and Ariane, the rebellious keeper of the
lonely lighthouse of Skellig Mor.

In the depths of an undersea cavern, Lily struggles
to communicate with the sea dragons and escape
the skeleton-filled tunnels beneath the lighthouse.
Only then can she complete her quest—to enter a
fantastical library that has existed from the
beginning of the world...